GIRLS
OF
THE
DARK
A DCI DANI BEVAN NOVEL

BY

KATHERINE
PATHAK

≈

The Garansay Press

Books by Katherine Pathak

The Imogen and Hugh Croft Mysteries:

Aoife's Chariot

The Only Survivor

Lawful Death

The Woman Who Vanished

Memorial for the Dead
(Introducing DCI Dani Bevan)

The Ghost of Marchmont Hall

Short Stories:

Full Beam

DCI Dani Bevan novels:

Against A Dark Sky

On A Dark Sea

A Dark Shadow Falls

Dark As Night

The Dark Fear

Girls Of The Dark

The Garansay Press

PROLOGUE

Edinburgh High Court, 1975.

The young lawyer picked up his files and quickly trailed his colleague down the corridor, having to jog to keep up. 'Do you want me to relay my findings as we walk, sir?'

'That won't be necessary, thank you, Irving. The client wishes to stick to his current plea. I happen to agree with him.'

'But his psychological profile has thrown up something interesting. I believe this information could help us to argue for mitigation.'

'There is no mitigation with an innocent plea.' The senior advocate delivered this statement with barely suppressed irritation, as if his assistant had failed to grasp even the basics of law.

'I know that sir, but if we were to *change* that plea, we could argue for diminished responsibility perhaps. We still have time and the prosecution are willing.' Jim Irving had managed to overtake the older man and was running backwards now, in order to catch his eye. 'The jury are hostile to Calvin. I can tell. I know there are a good number of black women jurors in the selection but I think it's irrelevant. They don't like our client. They believe he's guilty.'

'Developed the second sight now have we Irving? A wonderful talent in one so young.'

The two men had reached the double-doors of the courtroom. Pausing momentarily on the threshold, Anthony Alderton QC rested his palm on the handle. 'I am sticking with our current defence strategy. I've been handling murder cases in this building since before you were dribbling on rusks, boy. We are more than half way through the trial. Why on earth would I shift tack now?'

With that, he pushed his way inside, leaving the younger man standing alone in the near empty corridor.

'Because you're losing,' Jim Irving muttered under his breath. 'And you've taken a gamble that will cost a man forty years of his life.' The lawyer smoothed his robes and stood up straight, following his boss through the doors with a heavy heart.

Chapter 1

DS Alice Mann pinned an enlarged photograph to the board. 'This is Ray Kerr with his mother, Janet. The picture was taken at her fiftieth birthday party a couple of years back.'

'They look happy,' DCI Dani Bevan commented.

'Aye, Ma'am. Until they came into contact with Lisa Abbott, I believe they were. Ray was probably a bit lonely, but from what I can tell from talking to friends and family, he was perfectly contented.'

DC Andy Calder stepped forward with a few more glossy prints, which he attached to the board next to Alice's. 'And this is how the Kerrs look now. These shots were taken by the scene of crime techs. The pair were found in the sitting room. They'd both swallowed household bleach. They must have writhed around in agony for a while before death. The coffee table was up-ended and Janet had fallen to the floor. There were bodily fluids everywhere.'

Dani crinkled her nose in distaste. 'Is there any evidence to suggest that another person was present when they died?'

Andy shook his head. 'The techs don't think so. It's a double suicide, prompted by a phone call placed by Lisa Abbott to the Kerr household the evening before.'

'We can't know that for certain,' DS Phil Boag interrupted.

Andy grunted. 'I'm not sure what else would have caused an otherwise law-abiding, happy-go-lucky mother and son to embark upon such a particularly unpleasant suicide pact.'

'I'm just saying there's no evidence to show a

connection.' Phil's expression remained fixed. He was used to fighting his corner with Andy.

A number of the officers turned their heads as a tall man in a black suit stepped out of the lift onto the floor of the Serious Crime Division. He took a place at the back.

'Don't mind me,' he said amiably. 'Carry on with the briefing.'

DCI Bevan took over, addressing DCS Douglas directly. 'We are discussing the case of Raymond and Janet Kerr, sir. Their bodies were found by a neighbour in Janet's Anniesland home on Friday morning. They'd taken their own lives. From an examination of the phone records, along with the testimony of friends and family, it seems that the pair had been the unfortunate victims of an elaborate scam orchestrated by a woman called Lisa Abbot.'

'Was this woman extorting money from the Kerrs?'

Dani nodded. 'Yes, that was main objective of the scam. Mrs Kerr's husband was killed in action during the first Gulf War. There had been some compensation paid to the family and Janet received a widow's pension. It wasn't much, but Lisa Abbot must have got wind of it somehow.'

The DCS tutted loudly. 'A nasty case. I don't suppose we can get a charge to stick over the suicides?'

'No sir,' DS Mann supplied. 'The best we can hope for is a charge of fraud and extortion. It looks as if Ms Abbot has been up to these tricks before. We are currently searching for other victims.'

'Good. Keep it up.' The man flicked his gaze towards Dani. 'Could we have a word?'

Bevan led her superior officer to her tiny corner office, allowing him to enter first and then pulling the door closed. 'What can I help you with, sir?'

Ronnie Douglas eyed her carefully. He was aged in his early fifties and possessed a thick head of dark hair, with a dash of white at the temples. The man was tall and well-built, giving him considerable presence. But a reputation for rarely cracking a smile had earned him an unfortunate nick-name at the station. 'I see that you've applied for the vacant superintendent position?'

'Aye, sir. Angus Nicholson had been encouraging me to go for promotion, even before he had his stroke.'

Douglas kept his countenance steely.

Dani decided she had no chance of being able to work out what the guy was thinking.

'It would be a shame to lose you from my team so soon. But I understand your desire to progress. I will have to start considering a replacement. I may need to bring in a DCI from another division.'

Dani raised her hand, as if she were slowing speeding traffic. 'It's early days yet. It will be a week or so before the short list is even published. I want you to know that I'm absolutely committed to my job here. This team means a great deal to me.'

The DCS gave an almost imperceptible nod. 'I don't doubt it does. But I need to think to the future. That is what management is all about.'

Dani had opened her mouth to say something more when Douglas delivered a curt goodbye and swept out of the room. The DCI was left gawping at his retreating figure, wondering if this was just a taste of things to come.

Chapter 2

'What did 'dour' Douglas want?' Andy placed the glasses he'd been balancing precariously between his fingertips down on the table.

'You need to get out of the habit of calling him that. Otherwise you'll end up saying it to his face.' Alice reached for one of the pints, nodding her thanks.

'That's what *I* keep telling him.' Dani sighed, knowing that Andy Calder was unlikely to take advice from anyone present, least of all Alice.

Calder smirked, gulping down his lager. 'I reckon it's an act. The guy knows exactly what his station nickname is. But it doesn't answer my question. What was the big fella after?'

'The DCS is starting to consider who should be my replacement. *If* I get the superintendent job.' Dani sipped her white wine. Her gaze slid across to Alice. She knew the girl was ambitious. But the young DS had kept her expression blank.

'That's a bit premature, isn't it?' Andy looked genuinely surprised. 'We haven't even got a DI in our unit. Phil's still going through the assessments. If Douglas wants to replace you, he'll have to bring someone in from outside.'

'I don't like the sound of that,' DC Dan Clifton added. 'We haven't got used to the new DCS yet.'

Dani smiled encouragingly. 'Come on, I don't know if I'll actually be shortlisted. Like Andy said, this speculation is a bit premature.'

'No offence, Ma'am,' Dan continued. 'But there's not a chance in hell you won't be on that shortlist. There can't be more than half a dozen female officers as senior as you. The Chief Constable would be terrified of the repercussions if there wasn't a woman being seriously considered for the job.'

'That's all well and good.' Alice polished off her pint, leaning forward to emphasis her words. 'Plenty of female DCIs make it to the interview stages for the top positions. But the evidence shows that they don't then get selected. It's the glass ceiling in operation.'

'I've not come across any barriers to my progression so far,' Dani clarified. 'But I'm moving in new circles now. I've no idea what to expect. All I can do is hope that my record speaks for itself.' She finished the wine and stood up. 'Thanks for the drink, I'm heading off now.'

'Do you want a lift, Ma'am?' Andy glanced up.

'No, thanks. You stay and have another. I'll see you all first thing.'

*

James had made dinner. When Dani arrived at her Scotstounhill flat she was surprised to find him already seated at the dining table eating it.

'Oh, sorry, I didn't expect you home so soon. I left yours in the pot.'

Dani smiled. 'Not a problem, I'll freshen up then come and join you.'

James busied himself setting another place at the table and pouring his girlfriend a glass of wine. She returned to join him a few minutes later, wearing a robe and with her damp, closely cropped hair enclosed within a carefully coiled towel.

'Thanks,' Dani said, placing a kiss on his lips and slipping onto the chair opposite. 'This looks great.'

'Good day?' James leant his elbows on the table. He was still in his work clothes, but his tie had been discarded and his sleeves rolled up.

'We've been assigned this nasty double suicide in Anniesland. It seems as if the pair were being blackmailed by a con artist.'

'Is that the mother and son? I heard the story on the radio. It was tragic.'

Dani nodded, her mouth full of food.

'The reporter made it sound like the man had learning difficulties.'

'I'm not sure that Ray had a proper diagnosis. He'd lived with his mother until this Lisa Abbot came along. Ray worked at one of the local garages. He was perfectly independent and capable of taking care of himself. But his school records show he was of below average intelligence.'

'Do you think the woman targeted him for that reason?' James drank his wine.

'Probably, *and* the fact that Janet had a healthy widow's pension from the army. She'd received compensation when her husband was killed in 1991. Most of the money was still in her bank account.'

'This Lisa Abbot woman had certainly done her homework. Has she got previous convictions?'

Dani shook her head. 'Not for fraud or deception, but we're certain this isn't the first time she's extorted money from folk. Alice is trying to track down Abbot's other victims. We've got surveillance on her flat right now.'

'I hope you throw the book at her. These people are the lowest of the low – preying on the vulnerable. It's not like the Kerrs had much money to start with.'

'It's worse than that. This scheme involving Ray and Janet was complex. It was almost as if Lisa was involving them in her twisted fantasy life. She seduced Ray and persuaded him to purchase a flat for them both, then Lisa told him she had to live there alone, because a previous boyfriend was violent and would attack her if he suspected she was co-habiting with a new man.'

'Sounds bizarre.'

'Oh, it gets weirder. Lisa would regularly call Janet and Ray, pretending she was a policewoman who'd been given the job of protecting Lisa from her ex-lover – like a kind of liaison officer for battered women.'

'What was the purpose of that? The Kerrs could have recognised her voice and the whole scam would have been blown sky high.'

'To lend credence to the story, I suppose. But the woman took lots of unnecessary risks. Lisa had full use of the flat Ray had bought, but she wanted more. She claimed the violent ex-partner was demanding money from her. Lisa had run up debts before leaving him and he'd had to pay them off. Now he wanted his cash back.'

'So Ray gave Abbot the money, to pass onto her imaginary ex-lover?'

'Yep. It amounted to £5,000. Ray had put down a £10,000 deposit on the flat and was fronting up £850 a month in rent.'

'What pushed the Kerrs over the edge? Had Ray given away all their savings?'

'We aren't totally sure yet. Lisa made a phone call to the house on the evening before the suicides, but we don't know exactly what passed between them. The rest of the information we've got comes from Janet's sister. She'd been told everything about what was going on and recognised that Abbot was scamming them. She couldn't persuade her sister, though. Ray and Janet were totally in thrall to Lisa Abbot.'

'Did you see the bodies?'

'Fortunately not. It was Andy and Alice who went to the scene. Andy was really upset by what they encountered there, especially the state of the mother. He's out for blood.'

James stared down at his plate, his appetite suddenly gone. 'You won't be able to charge her in connection with the suicides. But with some othcr victims prepared to testify in court you may secure a decent sentence for fraud and blackmail.'

'I sincerely hope so. That woman is responsible for those deaths. Just as if she'd held the pair down and poured that awful stuff into their throats herself.'

Chapter 3

The atmosphere in the city morgue was sombre. Dani supposed it always was, but there was something about the pathetic state of the Kerrs' bodies that made those present particularly subdued.

'There is significant scarring to the oesophagus, stomach and duodenum, as you can see. This was caused by the corrosive nature of the chemicals consumed.' Dr Culdrew paced up and down beside the metal table upon which Janet Kerr's body was laid out. 'Mrs Kerr didn't manage to consume as much bleach as her son, so death was more prolonged. There is bruising evident to the arms and shoulders, where she writhed about on the floor before falling unconscious. From the scene photographs, I surmise that Mrs Kerr struck the coffee table several times as she thrashed about.'

'Is it possible that a third party caused the bruising?' Dani pressed the mask close to her mouth.

'Anything is possible, as you know. In this case I'd say not. The bruises are consistent with the blunt corners of the solid wood table. There are no scratch or punch marks, which we would expect with a physical attack. As the body ages, the skin becomes thinner and bruising more apparent. Mrs Kerr is simply a person who bruised easily.' Culdrew pulled off his plastic gloves and led the officers out into the corridor. 'My *post-mortem* in both cases supports a finding of suicide. I'll pass the report onto the Fiscal's office. It will be up to them to reach a final judgement.'

'Thank you, doctor.' Dani shook the man's hand.

Andy lingered for a moment. He'd worked with Culdrew before and knew he could be persuaded to speculate beyond the brief. 'Have you ever come across a case like this before, Rob?'

Dr Culdrew began to walk with them towards the wash-rooms. He sighed. 'Sadly, yes. It was many years ago now. A young girl accidentally swallowed household bleach. Her father had stored it in a lemonade bottle in the garage of their house. It was one of those terrible, tragic misfortunes.'

'Were the wounds in that circumstance consistent with what happened here?' Andy held the door open for his colleague.

'Yes, largely similar. The girl had not intended to kill herself of course. Her stomach was pumped at the hospital she was rushed to. Sadly, too much damage had been done to her internal organs to save the poor thing. Her heart gave out under the strain.' Culdrew went quiet as he scrubbed his hands under the tap.

Andy felt bad about bringing the memory back. However, they had a job to do. 'And was there bruising in the case of this girl – did she writhe about?'

Culdrew knitted his brow. 'Not that I recall. I'd have to dig out the notes again. Off the top of my head I'd say no.'

'Did the tox screens show anything of interest with the Kerrs?' Dani interjected, unsure of where Andy's questions were designed to lead the pathologist.

'There were moderate levels of alcohol in both systems and traces of barbiturates in Ray Kerr's blood sample. I'd put it down to as little as a sleeping tablet consumed the previous evening.'

'Can traces of a sleeping pill remain in someone's system for that long?'

'Oh yes, up to forty eight hours.' Culdrew wiped the water off the length of his arms with paper towels. 'If that's all detectives, I really need to write up my notes?'

'Certainly, we'll leave you to it. Thanks again for your help.'

*

'What's with all this interest in the bruising?' Dani glanced across at her partner, as he drove them back to Pitt Street.

'I just think it's odd. Why would one person thresh about so wildly and another simply conk out on the sofa, in the exact same position they were in when they downed the bleach?'

'Culdrew's scenario explained it. Janet Kerr hadn't consumed enough to die straight away. She had time to struggle. It must have been an awful way to go.'

'Maybe the alcohol and barbiturates in Ray's system made him more docile.'

'We'd need to have a proper look at the toxicology results. Culdrew didn't make it sound as if there would be enough for that. Ray was quite a big guy. Working at the garage had obviously kept him fit.'

Andy nodded, saying no more. He and Alice had been at the scene and his boss hadn't. There was something about what they witnessed there that possessed all the hallmarks of a violent crime. Calder knew this was just a gut reaction. If the evidence didn't fit, he'd have to shake the idea. But something was making him think there was another individual involved. Not just a voice at the other end of a phone.

Chapter 4

Lisa Abbot was listed on the electoral register for her district as being thirty two years old. According to Janet Kerr's sister, she'd claimed to be twenty eight. This was just one of the many lies that Abbot had spun over the previous few months.

Alice and Dan sat in an unmarked car outside the flat on Raven Hill Road that Ray had bought for them. Abbot hadn't yet emerged through the front door.

'Are both their names on the mortgage?' Dan asked casually.

'Yep. Abbot will probably get to keep this place whatever happens.' Alice lifted a flask from the cup holder and unscrewed the lid. 'Want some?'

'What is it?'

'Hot chocolate.' Alice poured a small amount into the plastic beaker.

'No thanks. I'm watching my weight.'

Alice laughed. 'What the hell for?'

'I'm sitting on my arse on surveillance jobs most of the time these days. The big-bottomed look isn't a good one in men.' Dan shifted about uncomfortably.

The DS twisted round to face him. 'Have you got a new bloke?'

'There's a guy I've been talking to at the Lime Tree. He seems quite keen. But he's a body beautiful type.'

'Great. I never meet anyone.'

'Come on Alice, you're not interested. Half the men at headquarters would go out with you like a shot. You're focussed on getting ahead. I just wish I had your ambition.'

'Are you going to take the sergeants' exam again? There's another set coming up in January.' Alice sipped her drink, carefully balancing the flask between her knees.

Dan sighed. 'I suppose so. I don't want DCS Douglas to think I'm a total numpty. I can't believe I failed it the last time.'

'The DCI wasn't around to motivate you. She was busy on that disciplinary thing in Edinburgh.' Alice nudged her partner's arm. 'Bevan isn't going to be with us forever. In a few months she'll have moved upstairs and won't be there to hold your hand. You'll have to start being more proactive about your career.'

Dan was about to answer when the communal door to the block of flats opened. A woman in skinny blue jeans and an oversized hoodie jacket emerged. Sunglasses were obscuring most of her face.

'Is it Abbot?'

'I think so.' Alice turned the key and started the engine, waiting until the woman was a good distance away before crawling along behind her.

'I'll get out and follow on foot.' Dan grabbed his walkie-talkie from the glove compartment and shoved it into his pocket. 'There you go, Sarge. That's me being pro-active.'

Abbot had headed for Anniesland station and took a train into the centre of town. The carriage was busy and Dan was able to follow her with ease. She finally stopped at a gastro pub in the west end, where Abbot joined a man seated by the window.

Dan took up position at the bar, ordering a bottle of beer. He wanted to blend in with the other lunchtime drinkers. Whilst keeping half an eye on his quarry, the DC considered Alice's words of advice. His heart hadn't been in the promotion to sergeant. He didn't know why Nicholson had put his name forward. He'd cocked up during a case several months before and a young colleague was killed as a result. Dan supposed if he was honest with himself, he'd have to admit he sabotaged his own chances in that exam. He barely revised for it and got hammered in the pub the night before.

The couple in his peripheral vision had raised their voices. The man was of early middle age and wore a nice suit. Abbot leaned in close to his face and was saying something under her breath. She finished her drink and stood up, leaving him at the table before storming out.

Dan let her go. He knew that Alice was poised to pick up her trail when she stepped into the street. Instead, he lifted his bottle and moved over to the seat their suspect had vacated. The man opposite stared at him in surprise.

Dan held up his warrant card. 'My name is DC Clifton. I'm with the Serious Crime Unit. Can you tell me what your business was with the lady who just left?'

'Sara? What's that got to do with the police? She's a personal friend of mine.' The man smoothed his shirt irritably. 'I really need to get back to the office.'

Dan could tell he was worried. 'That woman, who you know as Sara, is in actual fact Lisa Abbot. She is being investigated by our unit on several counts of fraud and deception.'

The man shot to his feet. 'This is outrageous!'

Half the pub turned to look at him.

Dan tilted his head. 'Has she asked you for money?'

The man remained standing for a moment longer before slumping back down again. 'Yes.'

'How much?'

'Four thousand pounds. But we've argued about it. I can't release those kinds of funds without my wife becoming suspicious.'

'Why did Ms Abbot tell you she needed it?'

'I can't get used to her being referred to in that way. Sorry, she needs it for her treatment. Of course I understand and I sympathise, but we only slept together a couple of times. I don't really see why I should be responsible for her healthcare bills.' He looked Dan straight in the eye. 'Does that make me an awful person?'

'No, sir. It does not.'

Chapter 5

'I'd say she's desperate. Lisa Abbot must know we're investigating her, yet she's still up to the old tricks.' Alice took the lead in the de-brief taking place in DCI Bevan's office. Dan was perched on the sofa behind.

'Who is this man and will he provide us with a signed statement?'

'His name is Nick McKenna,' Dan pitched in. 'He works for an insurance company in the city centre. McKenna met Abbot at a bar six months ago. She told him her name was Sara White. They've slept together a few times in hotels near McKenna's work.'

Dani looked up from her notes. She beckoned to the DC. 'Come closer, Dan. Sit at the desk and tell me the details. *You* interviewed the guy. Don't skulk about at the back of the room.'

He moved forward, suddenly self-conscious. '*Sara* informed Mr McKenna a couple of weeks ago that she was going to have a biopsy on a mole on her back. According to White, the docs said it was malignant. The cancer had spread and there wasn't much they could do. She then claimed that there was a new treatment for malignant melanoma being trialled in the United States. The drug programme would cost £4,000 pounds and she asked him to loan her the money.'

Dani frowned. 'Abbot must have been sleeping with this McKenna chap whilst she was carrying on with poor Ray Kerr.'

Alice spotted her opportunity to take up the story. 'It doesn't sound like Mr McKenna suspected the illness was bogus. But he was concerned that if he didn't give Ms White the cash, she would tell his wife about their affair. He stressed that Sara appeared desperately upset by her diagnosis. She even showed him the mole, which he thought looked abnormal.'

'Well, the man's no doctor, is he?' Dani rolled her eyes. 'This woman is a real operator. Will McKenna testify to this in court?'

Dan shrugged his shoulders. 'I'm still working on it. Right now, the man believes he's had a lucky escape. He does not want his wife to find out about the relationship. McKenna kept asking if we had other witnesses. I think he's hoping we won't need his testimony.'

'Did you inform him that our two other witnesses died a long, agonising death and their bodies are currently stretched out in the city morgue?'

'I did mention it, Ma'am, although perhaps not in those terms.'

'Well, I may need to have an uncompromising chat with our Mr McKenna. But in the meantime, keep evidence gathering. Ms Abbot is just too good at this. I bet she's been conning the more gullible folk of Glasgow for most of her life.'

*

The restaurant was on the top floor. Their table was positioned next to a bank of windows providing a panoramic view of the city. The lights of the buildings twinkled far below, under the darkening sky.

'We would never have been seated somewhere like this a couple of months back.' Linda Irving swept a napkin across her lap. Her tone one of incredulity.

Her son grinned. 'I know. Quite the little miracle,

isn't it?'

'James simply encountered a peril far greater than his fear of tall buildings,' Dani added, sipping from her glass of wine, '- a man pointing a gun at his chest. It tends to cure all the less rational of phobias.'

'It focusses the mind, that's all.' James sat back while the waiter laid down his starter. 'Are you okay, Dad? You've been very quiet since we arrived.'

Jim Irving dragged his eyes away from the view. 'Oh, yes. I'm fine. It's just been a tiring week, that's all.'

'Sally has got your father helping her out on a case she's defending. He's been ploughing through papers well into the night. I've told him to slow down. He won't listen.'

'What's the case?' James asked.

'Defending the indefensible,' Linda muttered into her gin and tonic. 'Just the kind of case Sally likes best.'

'It's the trial of Aaron Lister. The music professor accused of sexually abusing his students. It's been in the news a lot,' Jim clarified.

'The charges came out of operation Nightingale,' Dani explained. 'I know one of the officers who made the arrest. High profile convictions for historic abuse bring forward victims of other sexual predators. That's why the police get accused of witch hunts. We suddenly find ourselves inundated with allegations against all sorts of public figures.'

'It's the job of the detectives and the justice system to weed out the bogus claims from the genuinely injured parties.' Jim polished off his drink, gesturing to the waiter to produce another round.

'So that's what you're helping Sally with - finding the genuine victims amongst the time wasters?' James prompted.

'Something along those lines, yes.'

James looked at his father's face closely. He thought he certainly did look tired, ill, even. 'Great. The main course is arriving. Let's forget about work for now – especially if it's not even ours! – and enjoy this lovely food.'

Chapter 6

The mid-week late night was taking its toll. Dani was sipping her third coffee of the morning when the reception desk called up.

'You've got a visitor in the foyer, Ma'am.'

'Can you ask them to make an appointment?'

'The man says it's urgent. It's a Professor Morgan from the University.'

'Oh, okay. Please sort him out a pass and send him up, Mandy. He's a personal friend.'

'Certainly, Ma'am.'

Rhodri Morgan had trimmed his steel grey hair into a far neater style than when Dani had last seen him. Those bright blue eyes positively twinkled when they alighted upon the detective.

'Good morning, Dani. It's good to see you again. I'm sorry for stopping by unannounced.'

Dani stood up. 'Not a problem. I've been meaning to call you. I've just been out of Glasgow a lot recently.'

Morgan took the seat at the desk. 'You're a busy person, I know that.' He waited for Dani to settle before saying, 'I wanted to discuss something potentially delicate with you.'

'Oh yes?' Dani was intrigued. At the same time, she really hoped it didn't involve her late mother.

'It doesn't relate to the two of us – well, not directly.'

Dani had forgotten what a perceptive psychologist the man was. He could tell exactly what she was thinking. 'Go on.'

'I've been working with a client these past ten years. He is currently incarcerated at Garwood Park, over in Dumbarton.'

'The prison for those serving multiple life sentences without parole? I always think it sounds like a Scottish Trust property.'

'Well, it is certainly very different from conventional prisons. Those individuals who are serving indefinite sentences are considered too dangerous to have amongst the general prison population.'

'Because they cannot be bargained with by the staff - they have nothing to lose because the courts have decided they must remain locked up forever?' Dani narrowed her eyes. 'Some still do get out eventually, don't they?'

'As you and I both know, there is no such thing as *forever* in the British justice system. My client is called Calvin Suter. He has just celebrated his 65th birthday.'

Dani shook her head. 'I've not heard of him.'

'You probably wouldn't. His sentence began in October 1975, exactly forty years ago.'

'He must have been convicted of murder?'

Rhodri dug around in his briefcase, fishing out a file. 'There's a photo here of Calvin back when he was first arrested. The rest of the papers are the details of the trial.' He pushed them across the desk. 'Between 1972 and '74, four women went missing around the Kilmarnock area. They were all aged between 19 and 25, each disappearing after a night out in local pubs. The police had focussed their attention on a particular mini cab firm from early on in the investigation, Princely Cars. One of their vehicles had been identified in the vicinity of two of the pubs the women had visited on the evenings they went missing.'

'Calvin was one of the drivers?' Dani looked at his photo, which must have been taken when the man was in his mid-twenties. Suter appeared to be of Afro-Caribbean origin.

'Yes. He was questioned along with several others. Calvin was working on each of the evenings in question. The police claimed there were gaps in the timeline of who he'd picked up and dropped off on those occasions.'

Dani sighed. 'Why do I always suspect the veracity of 1970s policing - particularly where there's a black man involved?'

Rhodri smiled thinly. 'It was a contentious case. The victims were all white, young and pretty. Although they were by no means angels, the prosecution presented them as such during the trial.'

'Upon what evidence was Suter convicted?'

'He was the subject of a surveillance operation. The bodies of the women hadn't been found. The DCI in charge of the case wanted the girls returned to their families. Suter lived alone, in a one-bedroom flat in Kilmarnock. One night, he drove his cab out to the Ayrshire coast, to an area with rough shingle beaches and jagged outcrops of granite, extending far out into the sea. The man spent an hour standing on the beach. He smoked a cigarette and sat on a rock. When he returned to his car and left, the cops observing him stayed to take a look around.'

'I think I'm beginning to recall the case.' Dani nodded sadly.

'One of the DCs discovered that the rocks on the promontory led into a kind of cave. You had to squeeze through a narrow opening to reach it, but once inside, the rocks opened out into a large cavern. It was very dark in there, but one of the officers had a small torch. They walked several feet into the cave system, to a section which had been scooped out by the waves to form an underground room. That's where they discovered the bodies.

The women had been chained together and kept alive in there for several days. The tide hadn't reached that far into the hillside any longer.'

'They must have been terrified.' Dani let her eyes skim through the grisly details.

'All the women were sexually assaulted and murdered. The technicians picked over the scene. There was no DNA analysis back then. The location didn't lend itself well to fingerprint detection. But with Suter effectively leading the police to the murder site, a warrant was issued to search his flat and one of the taxi cabs that Suter was reported to use most regularly.

As you will see from the evidence list in your pack, items of women's clothing were found in the boot of the vehicle. Cheryl Moss's mother identified them as her daughter's. Suter spent several months on remand. The trial began on the 21st October the following year. By the Christmas of 1975, Suter was serving four life sentences, to run consecutively and with no consideration of parole for at least forty years.'

'On *that* evidence?'

Rhodri nodded. 'They wouldn't have secured a conviction these days. The Crown Office might not even have allowed the trial to go ahead.'

'So, you're telling me that Suter is due for release?'

'Yes. He'll be out on Friday. Calvin has been an exemplary prisoner. He took a degree in English Literature in 1988 and wrote a book on Samuel Taylor Coleridge a decade later. There were several attempts made to appeal the conviction, back in the early days, but each one was rejected.'

'Do you think Calvin killed those girls?' Dani

looked at her friend's face closely.

Rhodri took a deep breath. 'Yes, I think he probably did. But at the time of the murders, he was like a completely different person. Calvin didn't know the difference between right and wrong. He'd had an extraordinarily difficult upbringing. The real problem was that his defence lawyer based his argument on the premise that Calvin was innocent. Anthony Alderton QC was convinced that the police evidence was flimsy and there had been institutional bias against Calvin because of his ethnic origin. If the defence team had put in a guilty plea and then argued for diminished responsibility, Calvin would have been free twenty years ago.'

'What happened to Alderton?'

'Oh, he's long dead. But the second in chair was a young defence advocate called James Sinclair Irving.'

It took Dani a moment to put the pieces together. '*Jim* Irving?'

'That's right. Your partner is his son, am I correct?' Rhodri appeared a little sheepish. 'I didn't want to be presumptuous, but I thought you and the family would appreciate a heads up. Calvin isn't dangerous, of course. However, he is articulate and intelligent. I expect there will be some press interviews and articles. Calvin didn't want to generate any publicity for his case whilst the parole board were considering his release. But now...'

'Yes, I see.' Dani wondered if Jim already knew about this and that was why he was so quiet the previous evening.

'Jim Irving barely lost a trial after the Suter case. I expect he learnt a tough lesson from the process. Perhaps if *he'd* been in charge, Calvin would have had a better outcome.'

'I'm not sure the outcome was wrong, Rhodri. If

Suter was guilty of torturing and murdering those girls, then he got the right sentence. If I didn't think that way, I'd be in the wrong job.'

'I don't disagree with your logic, Dani. But I suspect that like mine, Jim Irving's perspective on the events would be quite different.'

Chapter 7

There were very few people left on the serious crime floor when Dani finally logged off the system. She noted that the overhead light had been dimmed and tutted at the petty irritations that cost cutting had caused.

As she raised her gaze, the DCI noticed a bulky figure standing in the doorway to her office. For a second, she wasn't entirely sure who it was. Then recognition dawned. 'Please come in, DCS Douglas.'

The man entered a little hesitantly. 'It's dark in here, Detective Chief Inspector.'

'The lights get turned down to power save at 7pm, sir. I've got a desk lamp. I simply hadn't realised the time.' Dani wondered why the DCS didn't know about the procedure. Surely he'd worked this late before?

'Of course. Clearly I don't notice it when in my own domain. Now, I'm keen to get an update on the Lisa Abbot case. You seem to have rather a lot of officers on overtime watching her flat?'

'Yes, we're evidence gathering. I sent you the update about Nick McKenna. It seems that Abbot has other victims.'

Douglas knitted his brow. His eyes appeared almost black in the fading light. 'That is all well and good, but this department focusses on *serious* crime. I suggest that if we can't substantiate a fraud charge within the next two days you should drop it. There's no chance of a murder conviction in relation to the Kerrs' deaths. I've read the *post mortem* reports very carefully.'

Dani was taken aback. Nicholson had never read

the evidence she sent him, only the precis she provided with her attachments. Perhaps she'd underestimated Douglas. 'Fine. Give me until the end of the week, sir. Then we'll either bring charges or push the case on to CID at Abbot's local station.'

'Good.'

Dani could have sworn that the faintest flicker of a smile might have crossed his lips.

He made to leave, turning back just before he reached the door. 'I came down to speak with you earlier in the day, but there was a man here.'

'Professor Morgan, he's on our criminal profiler database.'

The DCS frowned. 'We aren't considering a profile of Lisa Abbot? I really don't think we have the budget for that and I can't see the point.'

'No sir, it had nothing to do with the Kerr case. The Professor is an old family friend. He was discussing another client of his, a long-term inmate of Garwood Park.'

'Does this inmate relate to your current case load in any way?'

Dani opened her mouth to provide an explanation then decided against it. She shook her head.

'We'll say no more about it. But I don't look kindly when personal considerations find their way into one of my busiest departments, is that clear?'

Before she had a chance to respond, the man was gone, heading towards the lift at a brisk pace.

*

'The guy's an arsehole.'

James laughed, topping up Dani's glass with wine. 'You mean you've never encountered one of those in the workplace before? You've led a charmed life my dear.'

'Of course I have. Douglas is different. He's a *well-informed* arsehole. They are the most dangerous kind.'

'Very true. I always got the sense you were pretty much left alone at your rank, especially with your recent successes. It must be a shock to suddenly get micro-managed.'

Dani shifted along the sofa, leaning her head against his shoulder. 'It isn't even that. The man's just *weird*. Anyway, let's not waste any more of our evening talking about the DCS.'

'I quite agree.' James put down his glass and slid a hand up Dani's thigh, leaning across to plant a kiss at the base of her neck.

'Hang on, there is something else we need to discuss.'

James pulled back. 'Sounds serious?'

'It shouldn't be. Only, the thing that Rhodri came to tell me about, it involves your father.'

He looked puzzled. 'In what way?'

'I spent the afternoon researching it on the database.'

James leant in again, brushing his lips against hers. 'Naughty girl, no wonder you're in trouble.'

She put a hand to his chest, but couldn't prevent herself from smiling. 'Concentrate, will you?'

'Okay.'

'Rhodri was telling me about your father's first ever murder trial. You would only have been a year old at the time. He was second chair to Anthony Alderton, QC; later *Sir* Anthony.'

'The Calvin Suter case.'

'You know about it?'

'Of course. Dad was involved in the three appeals that followed Suter's conviction. The case was his great regret. You know - the one that haunts a defence advocate's career. Dad told Alderton that he had the strategy wrong. But the guy was high court royalty back then and Dad was new and inexperienced. His opinion held no sway.'

'But did you know that Suter will be released in two days' time?'

James blinked ferociously, the playful smile wiped off his handsome face. 'No. I didn't.'

Chapter 8

Morgan had only provided Dani with the bare facts of the Suter case. The investigation had been a lengthy one, with many officers involved.

It took until the April of 1973, when the third victim, Kirsty Glendinning, went missing after an evening spent at the West Side Bar in Kilmaurs that a witness came forward with the description of a light blue Ford Anglia, seen in the West Side's car park on the night Kirsty had been in there. The witness thought they caught sight of a woman get into it. He was convinced she'd climbed into the back seat, making him think it was a taxi.

The vehicle was traced to Princely Cars of Kilmarnock, although the call centre had no record of a pick-up from Kilmaurs that night. The detectives went back to the witness statements from the previous disappearances.

A sky blue saloon car was spotted driving away from the pub in Kilmarnock town centre where Cheryl Moss had been drinking, during the summer of '72. She was the second victim. The police finally had a lead.

But Dani was surprised to see that Calvin Suter, who had worked for Princely Cars since '71, did not tend to use the light blue Anglia when he was on duty. In fact, the owner of the mini cab firm told the police that the car had been unreliable and was in the garage at the times when both Moss and Glendinning were taken.

But the car provided the only real lead that the Ayrshire constabulary had. They began a surveillance operation on five men who had worked for Princely Cars during the dates in question. Dani was surprised they'd been granted the budget. She thought the evidence was thin.

Suter had already come to the attention of the officer in charge of the case, DCI Harry Paton. Calvin had a juvenile record for breaking and entering. He'd served three months in a youth detention centre.

In the summer of 1974, Calvin went to Jamaica for two weeks, to visit his grandmother who was dying. The detectives hadn't got the evidence to get a court order to keep him in the country. The focus for the surveillance teams fell upon the other drivers at Princely Cars.

On the evening of 12th August 1974, 21 year old Debbie Cane failed to return to her parents' house from a visit to a bar and nightclub in Irvine. According to the police reports, Calvin had returned to Scotland by this date, but their teams had been unable to locate his exact whereabouts until the 14th of the month.

DCI Paton claimed that this window of time was when Suter snatched and murdered Debbie Cane. It was two weeks after the disappearance of Cane that Suter appeared to 'lead' the police to the cave in which the women's bodies were kept.

There was a knock on Dani's door. She automatically shuffled the papers into a pile and shoved them back into the unmarked file. It was only DS Mann.

'Sorry to bother you, Ma'am. We've got something interesting on Lisa Abbot.'

'Take a seat, Alice.'

'DC Tait followed her to an appointment this morning. Abbot visited a health clinic on Maryhill Road. Tait sat beside her in the waiting room.' Alice cleared her throat. 'I know we don't have the jurisdiction to look at her medical records, but Tait got a glimpse at what the letter in Abbot's hand said.'

Dani sighed, having a nasty feeling about what was coming. 'We can't use it in court, but go ahead.'

'Lisa Abbot has an aggressive malignant melanoma. She's suffering from Stage three, inoperable skin cancer.'

'What she told Nick McKenna was true?'

Alice nodded. 'It looks like it. Her approach to McKenna wasn't a scam at all. It was simply a dying woman begging her ex-lover to give her money for the treatment that might save her life.'

'Damn it. There's no fraud then. It looks like DCS Douglas will get his way. We'll have to dump the case on Maryhill CID.'

Alice frowned. 'Just because one of her stories turned out to be true, it doesn't mean that the rest were.'

'I know that, but we've not got enough to charge her. Even if we do get to court, her defence will say Abbot's too incapacitated to stand trial. She may very well be by then.'

'Yes, but the fact she's so ill means that Abbot must be desperate for that money. I bet she did something to really turn the heat up on the poor Kerrs. *That's* why they committed suicide. Just because *she's* been given a life sentence it doesn't mean the woman can take her victims along with her.'

Dani could see that Alice was genuinely rattled. She was glad. It meant the young detective cared. 'I'm sorry. The DCS won't allow us to take this further. As you move up through the ranks DS Mann, you'll have to learn how to balance the pursuit of justice with the realities of modern policing. I know it's frustrating to leave an investigation incomplete.'

Alice nodded. 'Thank you, Ma'am. I think I understand.'

'Good. Now get onto DCI Tyler at Maryhill. Give him a decent overview of where you got to with the Abbot case. Send him all the files. Then you'll have done the best you could for those two victims.'

'Of course.' Alice moved slowly towards the door, her posture just a little more bowed than when she'd first come in.

Chapter 9

Rhodri Morgan's flat was on the top floor of a gentrified tenement building not far from Kelvingrove Park. Dani had been there for dinner once before, meeting Morgan's eldest son, who'd been visiting for the university holidays.

This time, the professor was there alone. 'I'm glad you came round to discuss the matter further. I felt I'd not had the opportunity to give you a proper picture when I dropped into your office. It was my fault for not providing any warning.'

Dani assisted her host to place the cups on a small kitchen table. 'I've got a new boss. DCS Nicholson had a stroke last month and had to retire. His replacement is rather strict about sticking to our allotted caseload during working hours. I can only really discuss this Calvin Suter issue when I'm off duty.'

'I understand. We have Department Heads like that at the university. It's a terrible shame because it stifles intellectual growth and debate. Complex cases, like that of Calvin's, help those who work in the justice system to learn to become better practitioners.'

'You have the academic's approach to policing. It's more about business and management at my end.'

Rhodri poured reddish tea from an oriental looking pot. 'But detective work is not about balance sheets and statistics. It is an intellectual puzzle, like any other. All the very best crime fiction teaches us this.'

Dani smiled. 'Andy Calder would agree with you,

although he'd never call himself an intellectual. He thinks that policemen should be free to police. But his attitude has meant it's been impossible for him to progress in the job.'

'How is Andy?' Rhodri put the cup to his lips. 'I haven't seen him since he was at the Infirmary.'

'He is totally recovered physically, but sometimes cases can really get to him. There was a recent double suicide, for example. Andy attended the scene. Afterwards, he was hell bent on finding someone responsible.'

'This residual anger suggests to me that he is still suffering from the trauma of his abduction. If he will agree to it, I would be happy to conduct a few sessions with him.'

Dani grimaced. 'Thanks. I'll ask him, but I can't imagine he'll be up for it.'

'Well, make the offer anyway. You never know.'

'Will you continue to see Calvin after his release?' Dani changed the subject.

'Yes, actually. It's entirely his decision but a good number of my clients wish to continue our sessions outside of prison. I usually adjust my fees accordingly. It would feel wrong to abandon a patient, just when they need my help the most.'

'Aren't they most in need when they're first imprisoned?'

'I didn't know Calvin back then. I can't comment on his particular case. But most of my patients are serving multiple life sentences. Often, they were no more than children when they were convicted and are coming out old men. They don't know how the world works. Freedom can be utterly overwhelming for them.'

Dani sipped the fragrant tea. 'I hadn't considered that. It does seem incredible that Suter has been inside a prison for over forty years. People have lived and died in that time.'

'Exactly. These lengthy sentences are more commonplace in other countries, like the US. But here, it is really not the norm. I suppose we should be grateful that capital punishment is no longer an option.'

'I've reviewed the evidence in the police files from 1975 and the subsequent appeals. I'm amazed the prosecution secured a guilty verdict on the strength of their case. Almost all of it was circumstantial.'

'I certainly felt the same when I took Calvin on as a client in the early 2000s. He's never confessed to killing those women in all these years, even though it would have granted him an earlier parole. That's unusual for a guilty man, especially one as talented and intelligent as Calvin.'

'The first appeal argued that the surveillance on Suter had been illegal and all evidence gathered from it was inadmissible.'

'Yes, but this appeal failed. The surveillance was deemed lawful because of Suter's connection to the blue Ford Anglia. A colleague of his at Princely Cars testified that Suter had a preference for the vehicle and had always chosen it over others - before it began breaking down, that was.'

'Was that witness ever a suspect?'

'He had solid alibis for three of the murders. The man had a wife and three children to vouch for his whereabouts.' Rhodri lifted an eyebrow. 'Did you know that single men are 75% more likely to be charged with a crime than a married man is?'

'Because it's harder for a single man to prove he was home alone and this is usually his only alibi?'

'Partly. Also, as a society we are naturally suspicious of men who live by themselves. Especially once they reach a certain age. They are treated with caution. Ordinary folk don't quite know what to make of them.'

'Does that go for divorced men too?' Dani glanced quickly at her host, hoping he wouldn't take offence.

'Oh yes, definitely. If a series of murders occurred within this area I would expect to immediately become a chief suspect, particularly as I hang about with convicted murderers and child molesters. Indeed, I'm considered an apologiser for them in some circles.'

Dani didn't quite know what to say to this, she sensed he was right.

'The second appeal was launched after another young woman went missing in the spring of 1978.'

'I read about this. She was called Sarah Martin, 26 years old. She was a secretary at a financial services company in the city centre. Sarah went missing after a night out in her local pub in the April of '78.'

'Yes, the pub was in Fenwick, just a few miles from Kilmarnock. She has never been found. We still don't know for certain that the girl is dead.' Rhodri rubbed his beard. 'Although, I think it's extremely likely she is.'

'The police searched the cave system where the other women's bodies were discovered and similar geographical features along the entire Ayrshire coastline. They found nothing.'

'There was no other evidence to link Sarah Martin's disappearance to the original Suter case except for the fact it occurred within the same vicinity,' Rhodri continued. 'This wasn't enough for the appeal judge. Calvin's conviction stood.'

Dani took a moment to finish her tea. The light was beginning to fade outside the impressive sash and case windows. 'If Suter was the killer, why did he choose to take the girls to that cave? It seems almost primeval as a choice of murder site.'

'Unlike many of my other clients, Calvin never admitted to the crimes. We weren't able to analyse the various patterns and motives involved. Like all these awful cases, the answer usually lies in the childhood of the perpetrator. Calvin was born in Montego Bay, Jamaica, in 1950. His mother was Jamaican and his father a Scottish businessman. His parents never married. In fact, William Suter already had a family back in Glasgow when he fathered Calvin. But Suter supported his son financially during the early years of his life.'

'Was his father the reason Calvin came to Scotland?'

'Not necessarily. Calvin's mother, Elesha, emigrated to Britain in the early sixties. She'd lost touch with William by then and was trying to make a better life for Calvin and her other children. Elesha had various jobs, all of them low-paid. The family were very poor. Calvin left school at sixteen with no qualifications.'

'Plenty of young migrant families had a similar story. I don't see how Calvin's experience could have made him into a serial killer.'

'There was something that came up in the background searches on Calvin performed by his defence lawyers. The details never made it into the original trial. I suppose they worried it might be prejudicial to an innocent plea.'

'Oh yes?' Dani leant forward with interest.

'As you probably know, Jamaica lies within the hurricane belt of the Atlantic Ocean. The island has suffered from severe storm damage over the years. In 1955, Hurricanes Charlie and Gilbert hit the island directly, causing terrible damage and many deaths. Near to Montego Bay is a rocky configuration of low-lying cliffs and coves.

A group of young women were fishing from the

beach there in '55, when the worst of the hurricane struck. They must have sought shelter in one of the caves. Local villagers discovered them the next day. All the girls were drowned, their bodies left washed up in the dark cave. The whole area was in mourning for weeks.'

'Calvin would only have been five years old when it happened.'

'Yes, but the story was probably passed down through the years, perhaps becoming more gruesome with each telling. For a young impressionable boy, it could have left an indelible mark.'

Dani frowned. 'I still think it's a stretch. We've no idea how well Calvin knew the story of what happened to those girls. The murders in Ayrshire were of an entirely different nature.' She ran a hand through her dark hair. 'Everything in this case appears to be circumstantial. It's hard to pinpoint any solid evidence one way or the other.'

Rhodri nodded. 'But in my world, there are no absolute truths. It's amazing what apparently trivial events can leave a powerful imprint on a young mind. It might be that there was another, more violent and sexual motive for the killings, but in the method of disposal, the story of those girls in the dark cave, at the mercy of the Atlantic, had given Calvin the seed of an idea.'

Dani shuddered. 'And the man gets out tomorrow?'

'Yes. In fact, I shall be there at Garwood Park to greet him myself. The gate will be opened at three.'

Chapter 10

'Thanks for coming with me,' Alice said awkwardly.

'Not a problem. I'm as unhappy with the situation as you are.' Andy slipped on his Ray Bans, as the late autumn sun bathed their faces in brilliant gold.

'We're doing this in our own time. I can't see how the DCI can be upset about it.'

'It's not Bevan we should be worried about - it's DCS Douglas.'

'Either way, we aren't really doing anything wrong.'

Andy Calder could understand her reluctance to keep digging into the Lisa Abbot investigation. Alice had much more to lose than him. He'd heard on the grapevine that she wanted to go for DI in the next round of exams. The woman had only been a DS for a couple of months. Talk about fast stream promotion.

The pair approached the front door of the unassuming house in Anniesland. It was still sealed off with tape. Andy stepped over the garden wall and pressed on the neighbour's bell.

A small, neatly dressed woman in her mid-sixties opened up.

Alice held aloft her warrant card. 'We're from the Glasgow Division, madam. Would it be possible to come in and have a chat?'

The lady shuffled backwards. 'I suppose so. But I've already spoken with an officer, several days ago now.'

'That's okay. We're just making sure that nothing's been missed.'

The woman led them into a narrow sitting room at the back. Andy noted how similar it was to the Kerrs' place. It made him shiver at the memory.

'I'm Kath.' She held out a veiny hand. 'Janet was a good friend of mine. I'd like to help. Any news on when we might be able to hold the funeral?'

Alice shook her head. 'I'm afraid not. That will be up to Maryhill CID.' She cleared her throat. 'They've taken possession of the bodies.'

The colour drained from the woman's face. 'It's just awful and so out of character.'

'What do you mean?' Andy chipped in.

'Well, Janet was such a level-headed person. She brought up Ray pretty much single-handed after Lenny died. That's nearly 25 years ago. You must be aware that Ray wasn't a totally *normal* young man. He was a bit slower than other folk. But Janet made up for his short-comings. She looked after him.'

'Did you ever meet Ray's girlfriend, Lisa Abbot?'

Kath made a face. 'Yes, she came and went. During the spring the girl was a regular visitor. As soon as Ray bought her that flat, she was barely here at all. I told my daughter that was all she was after. We'd not see her round again.'

'What about during the days leading up to the Kerrs' deaths. Did you spot Lisa coming to the house then?' Alice eyed her expectantly.

'I'm afraid I wasn't at home on the day it happened. My daughter was ill. I went over to her place in Paisley to help with my grandson.'

'What time did you return?' Alice felt her heart sink.

'It was in the evening. It must have been around 7pm.'

'Did you notice anything unusual?' Andy picked up the questioning. 'Were there lights on next door – a car parked outside – anything at all that caught your attention?'

Kath dropped onto the floral sofa and considered this carefully. 'It was almost dark when I walked up the path to my front door. The lights must have been on at Janet's. Otherwise, I would have been concerned. We look out for each other, you see. She was a widow and so am I.' The lady put a hand up to her face. 'Now, it was a Thursday, which is when the local paper comes. I get annoyed about it, because the lad who does our street doesn't deliver it until very late. Everywhere else receives their copies in the morning. Sometimes the items listed in the classified section are gone by midday and I do like to see what's available. It puts me at a distinct disadvantage.'

Alice sighed, wondering where this flight of fancy was going.

'I remember now, that I spoke to the paper boy. Or who I thought was him. He's a big lad and wears an oversized zippy top. That night, he had a cap on too. I saw him step off the path, coming away from Janet's door. I muttered that he was getting later every week with that paper and I'd have a stern word with his mother if he didn't get his act together.'

'What did the boy say in reply?'

'Well, now you ask me about it, he said nothing at all, just took off down the street in the direction of the main junction with the A82.'

'And you didn't tell the other police officers this, when they questioned you before?' Alice edged forward.

'No, because it wasn't unusual. Robin Gabbler *always* delivers those papers late. It's probably the only constant on this whole estate.'

'Why are you mentioning it now?'

'Because when the other policeman asked, it was as if what I told him didn't really matter. He and his colleague were ticking boxes. Janet and Ray had killed themselves, why bother too much with what *I'd* seen or not seen.' Kath leant in close, so that Alice could smell her minty breath. 'But you two seem to think it's more than that. I'm not wrong, am I? You suspect that someone else was involved in what happened to poor Janet and her boy. It makes everything that occurred on that evening take on a new significance.'

'We aren't making any assertions here, madam,' the DS stressed. 'There's no new evidence.'

'No,' she replied matter-of-factly. 'But you've got a feeling, haven't you - that the Kerrs may have been murdered? Well, I'll tell you something; so have I.'

Chapter 11

The Sunday papers lay strewn across the kitchen table of Dani's flat. James had the colour supplement open to an impressive, glossy centre page spread.

'I can't believe they got the story out so quickly.' He sipped his cup of espresso, unable to take his eyes off the photograph.

'The reporters must have done the interview weeks ago. They were obviously just waiting for Suter's parole to come through before going to print.' Dani leant over James' shoulder. The double page shot was of Calvin Suter seated at a desk in his cell. A laptop was positioned before him and bookshelves lined with literary classics provided the backdrop.

The journalist had even inserted a thumbnail picture of Calvin's book at the end of the text. Readers were informed that they could purchase a copy of it at a reduced price from the paper's online bookshop.

'Is that really a prison?' James's voice was dripping with incredulity. 'It looks like a study in a country house.'

'Garwood Park isn't your typical prison. The inmates there are serving very lengthy sentences. Many of them committed crimes before we were even born.' Dani slipped onto the seat next to him. 'I've been there once, to interview someone. There are extensive gardens surrounding the main building. The prisoners tend to the allotments. Many grow the vegetables that are served in the canteen. I'm surprised this particular paper is having any truck with the place. Their front pages are usually full of headlines claiming that a stint in a British prison is like going to a holiday camp.'

'Hypocrisy is nothing new to *Informing Scotland*. If the story sells papers, it will go into one of their rags.'

'Does your dad get mentioned?' Dani reached out to touch his hand.

'Oh yes. There is a whole paragraph on Sir Anthony Alderton and James Sinclair Irving. The tenor of the entire piece is that Calvin was the victim of the incompetent and institutionally racist criminal justice system of the 1970s.'

'There was absolutely no question of racial bias in Suter's trial. That wasn't the issue at all.'

'No, but either Calvin or the journalist interviewing him now thinks there was. Dad's being smeared as an incompetent and the police inspector, DCI Harry Paton, as a crypto racist. The upshot of the article is that Calvin's imprisonment was a miscarriage of justice. The man is a sensitive intellectual who was stitched up by a flawed system.'

Dani lifted her cup, cradling it in her palms. 'I bet Suter's planning to sue for compensation.'

'Well, I know a little about the process. In order to gain damages from Her Majesty's Government, Calvin Suter will either have to prove his innocence to another jury or claim that his case was handled so incompetently by the defence team that they are at fault for the guilty verdict.'

Dani sighed. 'Let's hope he opts for the former rather than the latter.'

James closed the paper decisively. 'I think that rather depends upon whether our Mr Suter actually killed those girls or not.'

*

Andy Calder read again through the witness statements. He found Kathleen Nevin's original interview. As she'd claimed, it read like a tick sheet; being made up of a list of one word answers. Calder made a point of noting down the names of the PCs who performed the house-to-house inquiries. He'd find a way to pass them onto Bevan.

Alice had jotted down Kath's description of the man she saw leaving the Kerrs' property on the evening they died.

Ideally, they would want to create an E-fit, but use of the software had to be signed off by the officer in charge of the investigation. The neighbour hadn't given them much to go on anyway. He'd been wrapped up in heavy clothing, a cap obscuring his face.

Calder had already given the Gabbler family a call. The paper boy swore blind it wasn't him. His mum backed the lad up, saying he was slumped in front of the telly with his tea on a tray by 6.30pm that night. If Andy were still on the case, he'd be putting all of his resources into locating this unidentified man.

A shadow fell across Calder's desk. He visibly flinched, sliding an arm surreptitiously over the papers in front of him. Andy twisted his neck. 'Can I help you, sir?'

'No, Detective Constable. I'm hoping it's me who can help you.' DCS Douglas pulled up a seat to join him.

'Oh, aye?'

'It's been three months now since your terrible encounter with the O'Driscolls. But the department counsellor tells me you're very well recovered?'

'I'm right as rain, sir.'

'Good. I'm pleased to hear it. Well done on your role in the Alex Galloway case, by the way. We should get a double conviction on that one.'

Andy nodded an acknowledgement. 'I was just

assisting the DCI, that's all.'

'Only it's come to my attention, whilst reviewing the staff files, that you've not put yourself forward for promotion in the last seven years. That's a long time, DC Calder. These days, it doesn't sit well on your record to appear to be coasting.' The man's face was devoid of expression.

'I'm happy being a detective. It's all I've ever wanted to do. I like interviewing folk and putting the pieces of an investigation together. The management side has never appealed to me.'

Douglas nodded. 'I understand. But times have changed. We have young recruits looking to move up through the ranks. There have to be positions freed up for them to fill. It's the natural progression of things within the force these days. It really isn't an option to simply stand still.'

Andy inhaled deeply. 'Look, sir, it isn't only that. I had a bad health scare a couple of years back and then this incident with the O'Driscolls over the summer. I suppose I haven't wanted to rush things. I've got a young family. It's important to them that I stay healthy.'

The DCS blinked several times. 'If it's a matter of fitness to do the job DC Calder, then you put me in a very difficult position. I need my officers to be in the peak of condition. You may have to rely on one another for your lives. I want you to think very carefully about your position here. If you're treading water and in your heart of hearts you know that another, more resilient individual could take your place then you should consider it your duty to step down.' The man rose to his feet, moving away from the desk before Andy could respond.

'*Jeez*,' he muttered under his breath, watching his boss walk towards the lift. 'What the hell just happened there?'

Chapter 12

Despite the November chill, Jim Irving could feel tiny beads of sweat springing to his upper lip. He'd rarely visited his son's workplace before, but he wanted to make sure he spoke with him out of earshot of his mother.

James' law firm were a big multi-national enterprise. The Edinburgh offices were their main base in Scotland. Dani's boyfriend specialised in commercial and contract law. There was very little overlap between James's work and that of his father and sister. The office that Jim was directed to was small but pleasant.

James stood up to open the door. 'Dad! I'm really glad you've popped by. Take a seat. I'll have coffees sent up for us.'

'Thanks.'

'Are you in town for any special reason?' James returned to his desk. He was genuinely interested to know and not at all put out by the unexpected visit. Corporate law operated at a much calmer pace than the criminal bar.

'I needed to cash some cheques,' he mumbled. 'But I could really have done that at the local branch.'

James knitted his brow. 'Is anything wrong?'

'Do you remember the Suter case?'

'Of course. It was your first murder trial. It took place the year after I was born.' James decided to leave it there and allow his father to explain things for himself.

'Suter was released on Friday. He'd served forty years, which was the minimum sentence stipulated by Judge Richards.'

'Back in 1975?'

Jim nodded.

'Is it a problem that he's out - did Suter bear a grudge against you or Sir Anthony?'

'Well, if the man didn't, he bloody well should have done.' Jim clasped his hands together. 'Alderton botched it. The evidence was weak and he thought we could get the charges thrown out. Suter was claiming he didn't kill those girls. He was reasonably convincing. So, my boss decided to pursue a plea of innocence. Our entire case was built around the assertion that someone *else* killed those women.'

'You think that Anthony Alderton should have persuaded Suter to plead guilty?'

'If we'd opted for a guilty plea, we could have argued for diminished responsibility. Calvin Suter had grown up in poverty. The father was absent and his mother had a series of boyfriends. I'd discovered that one of those men, who'd lived in the flat with Suter and his sisters for two whole years in the late sixties, had gone on to serve time for child battery and rape. We could have used it in court, perhaps got the sentence down to 15 years.'

'The man could have been out in eight. That would have been in, what – 1983?' James puffed out his cheeks. 'Bloody Hell. That's quite a difference.'

'Judge Richards was a liberal. He would actually have been open to considering Suter's difficult upbringing in his sentencing. Richards had been a Labour MP before taking his bar exams. He wasn't your typical 1970s geriatric old duffer in a cap and wig.'

'But the jury didn't go for your argument of innocence?' James ushered in one of the secretaries, who had entered with a tray bearing a large coffee pot.

Jim took his time pouring the drinks into both their cups, the task seeming to focus his mind. 'We were fortunate during the selection of jurors. There were two women of Afro-Caribbean origin and one Afro-Caribbean man. For some reason, Alderton was convinced they'd side with our defendant.'

James sipped his drink and grimaced. 'Why the hell should they? Talk about racial profiling.'

'Alderton wasn't the most progressive of men, although he really believed he was. His prejudices were entirely subconscious. I watched the jury carefully as the evidence was presented. It was clear to me that they were appalled by what happened to those girls. The case had a terrifying, almost nightmarish quality to it. "The girls of the dark", is how the senior policeman who discovered the bodies later described the murders in his memoirs. Those jurors had made their decision before anyone had even set foot in a courtroom.'

'I suppose the fact that Suter had led the police to the bodies was what sealed his guilt in the eyes of the public.'

'You recall the details then?' A flash of suspicion crossed Jim's lined features.

'You talked about it for *years* afterwards, Dad.'

He sighed. 'I suppose that's true. It was the worst defeat of my career.'

'But it wasn't really *your* defeat – it was Sir Anthony's. I bet he didn't lose much sleep over it.'

'That's where you're mistaken. I saw his expression when the verdict was read out. His face drained of all colour. I thought he was going to keel over. Alderton realised how wrong he'd been.'

'I expect it was professional pride rather than anguish for Suter himself.'

Jim shook his head sadly. 'If my career has

taught me anything, it's that we cannot ever see into another man's soul. I couldn't tell you which it was with any confidence.'

James gulped down his coffee. 'You mentioned that Suter's claims of innocence were fairly convincing. Do you believe he was guilty of murdering all those women?'

'I've heard far more compelling protestations of innocence from people who turned out to be as guilty as sin.' Jim rubbed his brow. 'The important thing is that Suter's guilt doesn't actually matter. The man had mitigating factors in his childhood that should have reduced his sentence. I've never said that Calvin deserved to walk free. But to serve forty years, when poverty and abuse had distorted his sense of right and wrong, well, it's simply barbaric.'

James sat back in his seat and considered this statement. Perhaps he'd been spending too much time with Dani lately, but the solicitor found that he simply couldn't agree.

Chapter 13

The DCI was absolutely seething. Dani was awaiting the first round of interviews for the superintendent position, but she just couldn't concentrate. Her vision had gone blurry with anger.

To make matters worse, she could see DCS Douglas strutting about the personnel floor, as if he owned the place. Dani desperately hoped he wouldn't be in the room with them. Heaven forbid the man was actually on the panel itself.

It turned out he wasn't, but the meeting still hadn't gone particularly well in Dani's view. She'd not felt as confident as usual. Her eyes kept darting to the windows in the partition wall, trying to catch a glimpse of her superior officer, wondering what the hell he was up to whilst she was safely out of the way.

As soon as the interview was over, Dani dived for the lift, which carried her straight down to the serious crime floor.

The DCS was nowhere to be seen. Perhaps her concerns had been misplaced.

Phil took a step towards her, a supportive smile on his face. 'How did it go, Ma'am?'

'I'm not sure. You know what these things are like.'

Phil did know. He'd passed the detective inspector exams the previous month but was now being subjected to a series of tough interviews and training days. Phil Boag hadn't shown much interest in promotion in the past, but his two daughters were getting older. Sorcha was at university now and Georgie in the sixth form at Newton High School.

Since splitting from his ambitious wife, Phil had been able to concentrate on his own career a bit more.

'Is Andy around?'

'I've not seen him yet, Ma'am. He's been working on something with Alice for the last few days. She might have a better idea of where he is.'

'Thanks, Phil. Ring me when he gets in, will you?'

*

Dani remained at her desk until the sun was fading to a deep auburn over the city's skyline. She was determined to be bang up-to-date with her paperwork. The DCI had sifted systematically through the reports of all their cases going back five years. For some reason, she sensed that Douglas might be trying to dig the dirt on her and the team. She wasn't going to give him the satisfaction of being able to find anything.

When there was a knock at the door, Dani was so engrossed in the files that she jumped. 'Come in!' She hollered.

'This is what you get up to in the Serious Crime Unit. God, it's sexier than I thought.'

'James.' Dani got up from behind the desk, moving round to plant a kiss on his lips. 'I wasn't expecting you. Has something happened?'

'You coppers always think the worst.' He slipped his arms around her waist. 'I had a meeting with a client whose office is in Cadogan Street, remember? I said I'd pick you up at seven and take you out for dinner.'

'Damn. Sorry, I forgot. This interview business has got me rattled.'

James crinkled his tanned brow. 'We can go straight home if it's been a tough day. I really don't mind.'

Dani shook her head. 'No, it will be good to have

an evening off. I've been staring at reports all afternoon.'

He pulled her closer. 'You need to relax more.' He nuzzled his face into her neck. 'I meant it when I said you looked sexy at your desk. Do those blinds close?'

Dani laughed. 'We're in the middle of the Police Scotland Headquarters!'

James leant across and twisted the cord on the blinds at each window, allowing them to drop to the sill with a sharp clatter. 'There's absolutely no one here. The lights were off when I got out of the lift. I nearly tripped over a wheelie chair.'

Dani returned his urgent kisses, ushering him over to the small sofa that only just fitted along the far wall of the tiny room. James pulled his shirt off over his head and Dani undid the buttons on her blouse. She had to admit, there was something very exciting and elicit about doing this here.

There wasn't enough room to lie flat. Dani climbed on top of James' lap and unzipped his trousers. She hitched up her skirt and manoeuvred herself onto his erection so that within seconds, she was rising and falling to a gently mounting tempo. A file sitting on the cabinet jammed next to the sofa fell to the floor, cascading loose sheets across the carpet.

James rested his hands on Dani's hips, pulling her firmly to him until he sighed heavily, letting out a groan as his head fell back against the cushions. She leaned forward and placed a kiss on his sweaty forehead, allowing the bare, glistening skin of their upper bodies to lightly touch.

'Bloody hell. That was good. I'm going to be dropping by your office more often.'

Dani let out a throaty chuckle, resting her face against his cheek. 'I had some emotional tension to work out.'

James was about say more when they heard a faint knock at the door.

Dani twisted her body round, rapidly doing up the buttons on her blouse.

'Danielle? Are you in there? It's DCS Douglas.'

'*Shit!*' Dani rasped under her breath. 'Just a second, sir!'

They sprang to their feet. James pulled on his shirt and ran a hand through his hair before helping Dani to pick up the papers strewn across the floor. James plonked down onto the seat in front of the desk just as Dani flicked the lock and wrenched open the door.

Douglas stood for a moment on the threshold, his inscrutable gaze slowly taking in the scene.

'Please come in, sir. This is my lawyer, Mr Irving. He's been looking over the prospective employment contracts the panel gave the applicants this morning. He arrived *after* seven pm, so our discussions have occurred purely in my *own* time.'

James put out his hand and beamed broadly. 'Very pleased to meet you, DCS Douglas.'

The Detective Chief Superintendent allowed his eyes to flit between them suspiciously. He eventually returned the handshake. 'You've found nothing untoward in that contract, I hope?'

'It's all perfectly straightforward. A couple of clauses might need re-wording. I'll be contacting your legal department about it.'

Dani remained standing, not feeling inclined to invite the DCS to sit down. 'Was it anything urgent, sir?'

'Oh, not really. I just wanted to find out how the interview went.' Douglas cleared his throat.

For an awful moment, Dani thought he might actually be blushing. 'It went as well as can be expected. We get the de-brief in a couple of days.'

'I'm as much in the dark as you are. I just wanted you to know that I've put in a good word for you with the DCC. The work I've seen from your team so far has been impressive.'

'Thank you. I appreciate that.'

Douglas hesitated for a second, shifting his weight from one foot to the other. 'Well, I'll let you get on.'

Dani flung the door wide. 'Good evening, sir. Thanks for dropping by.'

Almost as an afterthought, the DCS twisted his head. 'It was a pleasure to meet you, Mr Irving. Please don't keep DCI Bevan too late with all this legal talk. She's my star officer.'

'I won't.' James waited until the man had got into the lift to say, 'Jesus, that guy's done something to seriously piss you off.'

'He's trying to get Andy the sack.' Dani screwed up her face. 'Do you know what? As 'Dour' Douglas turned away from you, I could have sworn the guy had a massive smirk on his face.'

James stood up and took her hand. 'Then you must have been mistaken. Because you've told me dozens of times that he wouldn't even crack a smile for his own mother.'

Dani shook her head, as if trying to rid her mind of any trace of the DCS. 'I don't want to talk about work anymore. Let's go and find somewhere really expensive to eat. I'm absolutely bloody famished.'

Chapter 14

Calder had spent the previous day knocking on doors in Anniesland, trying to find a resident who saw the man Kathleen Nevin identified as leaving the Kerrs' place on the night they died. He hadn't had much luck.

Andy stepped out of the lift and headed straight for his workstation. Phil Boag was breathing down his neck to get a result on a series of arson attacks committed on commercial car lots to the east of the city. He sat down and dug the file out of the mountain of paperwork on his desk. He was determined to work through it by the end of play. He didn't want the DCS to be able to catch him out on any loose ends.

As predicted, Phil made a bee-line for him. 'Andy. The DCI has been looking for you. And how are things progressing on the Royston Road Garage fire? Are the tech results back in?'

'Yes sir, they e-mailed them to me last night. The focal point of the blaze was the boot of one of the cars in the lot. They found large concentrations of thermite, which apparently burns at very high temperatures. It would have smouldered slowly to begin with and then exploded in very intense bursts of heat. The fire was so hot, it engulfed the nearby vehicles. They were packed in tight.'

'The fire was caused by an incendiary device?' Phil pulled up a chair, looking puzzled.

'It seems so. The techs reckon it was constructed using over-the-counter fireworks. They contain a thermite mixture, like a black powder. The chemical has a high boiling point and is as cheap as chips to buy.'

Phil scratched his head. 'It's bonfire night in less than a week. You can buy fireworks by the bucket load in just about every corner shop in Glasgow.'

'Aye. It doesn't get us any closer to finding a culprit. The techs think that even a kid could've put the device together.'

'How did they get it into the boot? Were the car keys used?'

Andy shrugged his shoulders. 'There wasn't enough of the vehicle left to be able to tell if the boot had been forced open. But the manager admitted that they sometimes forget to lock all the cars. They're jammed in close together and most couldn't be driven out without moving the others, so they don't get into too much of a sweat about it.'

'What about the insurance. Does the owner benefit from the compensation money?'

'It was the first thing we looked into. The insurance only pays out scrap value on the cars. The fact they've admitted to leaving them unlocked at night means the whole policy might be invalid. The guy claims he's ruined. The other garages that've had fires tell a similar story. Insurance pay-outs don't make people rich - that's only on TV.'

'So, you'll be focussing your inquiries on disgruntled employees, folk who've been sacked, upset neighbours – that kind of thing?' Phil stood up.

'We've already made a start, sir. Dan has been going through their personnel files.'

'Good. Just drop in to see the boss for a second before you get started, would you?'

'DCS Douglas?'

Phil furrowed his brow. '*DCI Bevan.*'

'Oh, aye, of course. I'll do it now.'

*

'Andy, come in and take a seat.' Dani glanced up from her screen. She pushed a cardboard take out coffee cup towards him. 'I got you this on the way in. It's probably cold now.'

Calder lifted it up and took a sip. It was barely lukewarm but reassuringly bitter and sweet. 'It's perfect, Ma'am.'

Dani folded her arms across her chest. 'Has Douglas spoken to you again?'

'Not yet. I got the feeling he thought he'd made his point perfectly clear the last time.'

'What are you going to do?'

'There's not much I *can* do. I'll have to submit my name for the sergeants' exams in the New Year.'

'It's the DCS who has to sign off on it. I'll approve your application, of course, but the final decision is his.'

'If Douglas really wants to get rid of me, he'll find a way.'

Dani pursed her lips. 'So the DCS wants to be the new broom, eh? Getting shot of anyone not seen to be on the fast track. To be honest, I didn't think he was the type. I had him down as old school.'

'It might be coming from above. Nicholson never liked me much, but he wouldn't have gone against your decisions. The old guv believed in letting his senior officers run their own team. Perhaps Nicholson actually made an effort to protect us from upstairs meddling.'

Dani smiled. 'I didn't think I'd ever hear you speaking wistfully about Angus Nicholson. His health has really improved, by the way. Eleanor says they're spending a lot of time back in Dornoch. They may retire there permanently.'

Andy grunted. 'I'd better dust off my golf clubs. I might be joining them soon enough.'

The DCI's smile faded. 'Not if I can help it.' She

leant forward. 'I'm prepared to do what I can to keep you in the serious crime unit, but you've got to be honest with me. I've been trawling through all our case notes covering the past five years. I don't want Douglas gathering any ammunition against us. But if there's stuff going on I don't know about, I can't stop him from hanging you out to dry. Besides, I happen to know you hate golf.'

Calder took another swig from the cup. This time the contents were stone cold. 'Actually, Alice and I have still been digging around into the Lisa Abbot case. We felt that Douglas was premature in kicking the investigation into the long grass.'

'And that's what you were doing yesterday?'

'Aye.' He shifted about awkwardly, surprised that his actions were so transparent.

Dani sat back in the chair and clasped her hands together, resting them in her lap. 'Come on then. Tell me exactly what you've found out.'

Chapter 15

When Dani was led inside Rhodri Morgan's west-end flat, she was surprised to see he already had company. A smartly-dressed Afro-Caribbean man was seated at the table in the living room. His hair was cropped short and ash grey in colour. The DCI's initial impression of the gentleman was that he possessed an air of dignity and self-composure.

'Calvin, this is DCI Dani Bevan. She's a friend of mine and an excellent detective.'

Calvin Suter rose from his seat. They shook hands warmly. 'I'm very honoured to meet you Detective Chief Inspector.'

'Call me Dani, please.'

'Shall I make more coffee?' Rhodri enquired.

'Don't go to any trouble on my account. I'm sorry to intrude. I didn't realise that you would have a guest.'

'Oh, we've finished our session,' Rhodri explained. 'But I hope that Calvin will stay for a drink?'

'Yes, I'd like that.'

'Then so would I.' Dani sat at the opposite side of the table and wriggled out of her jacket.

Rhodri scooped it up and disappeared out into the corridor.

'You must already know who I am.' Calvin made the statement matter-of-factly.

Dani nodded. 'I read your interview in the Sunday papers.'

'Yes. I gave that interview several months ago. I had no idea the paper would go to press so soon after my release.'

'It maximises the publicity. They know what they're doing.'

'That's certainly true. I still have cuttings of the tabloid front pages devoted to me around the time of my arrest. Some contain barely disguised racism.'

'Is there a reason why you've kept them?' Dani eyed him carefully.

'The skewed representation of me in the press was one of the arguments used by my lawyers during the appeals – both of them.'

Rhodri re-entered with a tray of drinks.

Calvin reached for a mug. 'But they are also evidence for my new book.'

'Oh yes,' Rhodri said. 'I didn't know you were working on another publication?'

The man broke into a wide smile. 'It's my life story. I've been working on it for the last forty years.'

Dani sighed inwardly. James wouldn't be happy about this news. 'How far through the process are you?' She tried her best to sound cheerful.

'Very close to the end, Detective Chief Inspector. I need to be careful to keep within the bounds of my probation criteria. But the rules with respect to creative endeavours are broader than you might think.'

'How far are you going to go into the circumstances of the murders?' Dani sipped from her cup.

'Will this book be a kind of confession, you mean?' Suter's face became inscrutable. 'Absolutely not. I barely recognise the young man who was accused of those crimes. He may as well be another person. I will be examining his role in the events as what you might call; an *interested observer.*'

Dani glanced at Rhodri, whose expression was grim.

'Ah, I see you don't think this is such a good idea,

Professor Morgan.'

'It's none of my business Calvin. But if you want my opinion I don't. You need to move on from your ordeal, start afresh. If you release a book about your life it will unleash a flurry of publicity. The families of the victims will suffer greatly. In many circles, you will be considered unfeeling and mercenary.'

Suter's posture stiffened. 'So I should just scuttle off into obscurity, be grateful that the British justice system finally decided to release me after *forty* years of imprisonment?'

'You're angry, which is perfectly natural. But the only person this emotion can hurt is you.'

'I thought our session was over, Professor?' Calvin managed to crack another grin. 'You are a wonderful psychologist Rhodri, and understand the many methods us weak men have for self-punishment. Perhaps that is exactly what my book is about. But it will still be written. I owe it to that young, ignorant, ill-educated boy who drove taxis for a living all those decades ago. His story should be told and that of all the self-serving careerists who conspired to take his future away.'

'There were people who tried to help you, surely?' Dani leant forward. 'Two separate appeals were launched and every effort made to overturn your conviction in those instances. The police don't deliberately set out to frame innocent men.'

Calvin drained his mug and stood up. 'I'll leave you two in peace. Thanks for the drink, Rhodri.'

'No problem, Calvin. I'll see you to the door.'

The man turned back to address Dani. 'It was a pleasure to meet you, *detective*. I hope my comments didn't offend you. We come from entirely different worlds, you and I. If it wasn't for the education I received in prison, I would never have come into contact with someone like you socially. But now I have been given that education *and* the notoriety of my conviction. Don't you see that I have a duty to use it?'

Dani nodded solemnly. 'Actually, I do.'

*

Morgan returned a few minutes later. 'What did you think of him?'

'He's articulate, polite and persuasive. I liked him. Unfortunately, he has the power to make life very difficult for James's family. The worse thing is, I can really see his point of view.'

'I thought you would comment on the way he has totally disengaged himself from the young man he used to be.'

'That makes sense to me if he's guilty. Calvin can claim it was a different person who killed those girls back then – not the man he is now.'

Rhodri nodded. 'Or, it is simply as he says; that the education he received in prison changed him on a fundamental level.'

Dani sighed. 'If being a police officer has taught me anything, it's that people don't change, not really. They can wear better clothes, talk differently and completely jettison their previous lives. Deep down they're still the same. It just takes an unsettling event to strip it all back. Then we see the essence of that person revealed. The Calvin Suter who was convicted of killing those girls back in 1975 still exists. He lives and breathes within the man who left this flat a few moments ago.'

Chapter 16

Andy was about to leave the building for the evening when he received a call from reception.

'I've got a lady on the line for you, DC Calder. She said you handed her a card a few days ago - when you were knocking on doors along Maryhill Road?'

'Put her straight through, please.'

A distant voice crackled onto the line. 'Detective Calder? It's Mrs Livingstone, from number nine?'

'Aye, I remember. How can I help?' Calder's heart began beating a little faster.

'I don't want to waste your time. I expect you know more about it all than I do. It's just that you were talking about Kath a lot when we spoke the other day. It seemed like a huge coincidence. Well, an awful one, of course.'

'What did? I'm sorry, Mrs Livingstone, I don't know what you're talking about.'

'Kath Nevin. She was knocked down yesterday afternoon near the bus stop on Western Avenue. Kath told me herself that her car was going in for a service. But it was the day she picked up her wee grandson from school. She'd have trekked through deserts to do that. So Kath was taking the no. 7. It's a busy road and a car hit her straight on as she crossed. The poor woman passed away from her injuries last night.'

Calder was silent.

'Oh, I hope I've not broken a rule by ringing a detective about a traffic accident.'

'No, Mrs Livingstone. Thank you for calling. I didn't know about this. If you hadn't taken the time to pick up the phone, I might never have done.'

'You didn't think to treat the death as suspicious?' Andy's tone was dripping with sarcasm, his face crimson with barely controlled fury. 'Kathleen Nevin was the Kerrs' next-door-neighbour, the last person to see the pair alive *and* the one who observed a suspicious man leaving their property on the night they both died.'

'We were only told that little nugget of information yesterday, *DC* Calder,' the sergeant at Maryhill put in.

Alice decided to intervene. 'You shouldn't have needed it to make a connection, Tom. Has a *post mortem* been carried out on Kath's body?'

The man shook his head in frustration. 'Her next of kin don't want one. The old lady was knocked down. What the hell is carving her up going to reveal to us?'

'Please tell me you've at least recorded witness statements from the scene?' Andy looked on the verge of taking a swing at the DS.

'Aye, the PCs who attended the 999 callout spoke to the folk in the queue at the bus stop. The car was speeding, they said. One old fella claimed it was a woman at the wheel, although he wasn't certain. She failed to stop then ran a red light further along the street.'

'We might have the car on camera at the junction.' Alice whipped out her phone. 'Did anyone get the make and colour – a registration number?'

DS Werner shook his head, snatching a glance at Calder, clearly worried he might be about to receive a thump. 'The witnesses didn't give the PCs much to go on.'

'Did they take names and addresses – so that one

of your team could follow up with a more formal interview later?' Calder threw up his hands. 'Actually Tom, forget I asked. I've got a feeling I know what your answer will be.'

'Just send everything you've got over to Pitt Street straight away, would you?' Alice put this request in a more amenable tone than her colleague.

'Does DCS Douglas know about this?' Tom Werner shot back, 'because he was very keen to have this case handled over here in Anniesland.'

The mention of the DCS's name made Andy's vision go blurry with rage. He took a step closer to the detective. 'Douglas doesn't know yet, but if you've got any plans to tell him then I'd think again, pal. You know I'm the guy who was kidnapped by those psycho killers a few months back?'

Werner nodded, beads of sweat having broken out on his upper lip.

'Well, it's left me with some residual anger management issues. Understand?'

Alice took hold of Calder's sleeve, dragging him towards the exit doors. 'I think he's got the message Andy,' she muttered darkly.

Chapter 17

Despite having seen her mug-shot, Lisa Abbot wasn't quite as Dani had expected.

The woman was diminutive in stature, her hair a mousy brown, falling straight to her narrow shoulders. Abbot's skin was pale and pasty. Dani wondered if this were because of her illness.

Abbot stood back from the door to allow the female officers to enter. The DCI had decided it wasn't wise to allow Andy to perform the interview. They were on thin ice as it was, cutting in on Maryhill's jurisdiction.

'Thanks for agreeing to speak with us, Miss Abbot,' DS Mann said kindly. 'We don't wish to keep you long.'

Dani let her eyes skirt over the small but modern flat. It was nicely decorated. A newly fitted kitchen was visible through a set of folding doors leading off the living room.

'The flat is only half mine,' Lisa explained, obviously noticing Dani's interest. 'That aunt of Ray's has got her lawyers onto me. She wants me to sell up and give her half the cash. She's the one who benefits from the will, you see. But I'll need a decent place to live in while I'm having my treatment. I hope to fly out to America in a couple of weeks.'

'And how is that trip being funded?' Dani asked as gently as possible.

Lisa narrowed her eyes. 'My friends have clubbed together. They've been very sympathetic, what with my diagnosis coming alongside the death of Ray.' She pulled out a dirty tissue and dabbed at non-existent tears. 'Why are you talking to me again? Do

I need the duty lawyer, like last time?'

'That really shouldn't be necessary,' Alice soothed. 'It's just that some new evidence has emerged.' The DS slipped an E-fit photograph out of her bag, having received the go-ahead from Maryhill to have one generated from Kath Nevin's description. 'We now have a witness who saw this man leaving the Kerrs' property on the evening they both died. Do you recognise him?'

Lisa peered closely. 'No. It could be anyone. Nobody killed Ray and Janet – they topped themselves. Why are the police still bothered about it?'

Dani had to take a deep breath before she spoke. 'Because it isn't always necessary to place your hands around someone's throat or plunge a knife into their chest to kill a person. It can simply take the right sort of lies and manipulation to leave a vulnerable individual feeling as if they have no option but to end their own life.'

Lisa sat up stiffly. 'I think I do need that solicitor. I'm not well, Detective Inspector. The stuff you're saying is upsetting me.'

Alice put up her hand. 'Okay, we'll leave you in peace.' The pair stood. 'Just one more thing, Lisa. Did you know that the neighbour who saw this man leaving the Kerrs' house on the night of their deaths is now dead too? She was struck down in a hit-and-run a few days ago. Not far from this flat.'

The woman coughed weakly. 'That's terrible news. They say that bad things come in threes. Let's hope that's the end of it, eh?'

Dani said nothing, curling her top lip in disgust. Then she glanced over Lisa's shoulder at the bank of photos on the windowsill. Most of them were of the woman alone, posing sexily for the camera, in times when she was healthier and more attractive. But in one shot, its frame tucked behind the others, a man was standing beside Lisa, an arm placed firmly around her waist. It was hard to make out his features, as the picture was predominantly in shadow. The DCI was pretty damned certain it wasn't Raymond Kerr *or* Nick McKenna.

*

Dani had given Alice instructions to dig deeper into Lisa Abbot's past. The photograph she saw briefly in the flat appeared to have been taken some time ago. Lisa's hair was longer and bleached golden by the sun. The tan sported by Abbot and her companion was deep and dark - the type that could never have been obtained in even the best of Scottish summers. If the man posing with Abbot in the shot was the same person seen leaving the Kerrs' house, she may have known him for many years.

The lights were off in the DCI's office, but as she approached, Dani could make out a figure seated at her desk. She swung open the door and allowed it to bang against the partition.

'Can I help you, sir?'

'Come in and take a seat, Danielle.'

Dani resisted the urge to close the door, leaving it wide open to the serious crime floor.

DCS Douglas leant forward ominously. 'I've been looking for you all morning. I took the liberty of having a seat in here, just in case I missed you.'

'I've been interviewing a witness.' Dani decided to elaborate only if pressed. Her eyes scanned the desk in front of her. She was wondering if anything incriminating had been left out in full view.

Douglas followed her gaze. When their eyes met, Dani could have sworn the man gave a half smile. 'I wanted to intercept you before you left the building in order to deliver the good news. The panel were very impressed by your interview. The DCC has put your name on a short-list of three candidates. The e-mail should be in your inbox now.' The man stood up and swept around the desk. He put out his hand, which Dani took reluctantly. 'Well done. It seems as if we are one step closer to that promotion.'

'Thank you, sir.'

He withdrew his hand and paused for a moment in the open doorway. 'I'm extremely confident that you will become the first female superintendent at Pitt Street. The final interviews are in two weeks. We just need to make sure that everything runs smoothly until then.' His expression hardened. 'It would be a tragedy if anything was to rock the boat in the meantime and such a wonderful opportunity was cruelly taken away from you.' With that, he was gone.

Chapter 18

Sally Irving Bryant QC returned to her offices after a long day in court. Her appearance was usually immaculately tended, but on this particular evening she was showing every one of her 52 years.

There was still a light on in the research room. Sally dipped inside the doorway to turn it off. She paused, with her hand resting on the switch. '*Dad*? Is that you?'

Jim Irving glanced up from a pile of papers. He was seated at the long table which dominated this mini library. 'Hi Sally. How did the hearing go?'

'Fine. We've secured bail for Aaron, although he'll struggle to raise it.'

'How much?'

'Half a million pounds.'

Jim whistled. 'How's he going to find that? He's only a retired teacher.'

'We've suggested he re-mortgage his Edinburgh house. It's trebled in value since he bought it, umpteen years ago. He can release the equity.' Sally shrugged off her gown and sat beside her father. 'It's better than custody. The trial could be weeks away yet.'

'I'm going through the testimonials that the prosecution released to you. We need to have detailed rebuttals for each of the allegations made by Lister's ex-students. We'll have to ascertain exactly where Aaron Lister was and who he was with on each and every one of these occasions he's accused of abusing them.'

Sally laid her hand on his arm. 'I really appreciate your help, but I've got clerks to do this for me. I don't want you wasting your evenings on it. Go home to Mum. She'll have made dinner.'

Jim shuffled the papers back into the files. 'I thought you wanted my input?'

'Of course I do. Your advice is invaluable to me. I just didn't think you'd throw yourself into things quite so energetically.' She smiled ruefully. 'I'll get into trouble with Mum and James at this rate.'

Jim shook his head. 'You're right, Sally. I should get going.'

Sally kept her hand firmly in place, as if tethering him to the spot. 'Is there something the matter? You aren't your usual self.'

'Have you spoken to your brother?'

'No, we've both been busy. What's going on?'

Jim slumped back down into the chair. 'Calvin Suter has been released from Garfield Park. His forty years was up.'

Sally was silent for a moment. 'I didn't know that. I'd been so wrapped up in the Lister case I'd not been keeping up with the latest news. Well, we knew it would happen eventually, Dad.'

'Yes, but his release has brought it all back, that's all.'

Sally suddenly got up, disappearing from the room for a few moments and returning with a bottle of single malt and two tumblers. 'Here, have some of this.' She poured a couple of generous measures.

'Dani knows Suter's psychiatrist. She says he's planning on writing a book. He's already given a candid interview to one of the broadsheets.'

'I actually remember the case well.' Sally took a slug of the whisky. 'I was still in the prep school back then. I was twelve years old. It's an impressionable age. The girls in my dorm were all horrified by the discovery of those women's bodies in the cave. It kept a few of them up in the night for a while. I remember Matron scolding us for listening to all the gory details on the Radio and TV news reports. We couldn't help it. The story was compulsive viewing.'

'Every single one of the jurors at the trial knew all the gory details too. We were fighting a losing battle.'

Sally swirled the liquid around her glass. 'Mum had not long brought James home when the trial started, do you remember? I felt really quite put out for a while. I'd been your only child for all those years.'

'You never resented him, did you?' Jim turned toward his daughter, an expression of surprise on his face.

'No,' she laughed. 'He was so sweet. And I knew how long you and mum had waited for another child. It's not something I share – the desire for children that is, but I do understand it. In many ways, I think that James was my baby too. I got to hold him and take him out for walks in the park in his pram. Maybe that's why I've never wanted one of my own. I got it out of my system with him.'

'There was never such a loved little boy,' Jim lamented quietly. 'I expect we spoilt him rotten between us.'

Sally chuckled, finishing off her drink. 'Yes, but it's done him no harm. It simply made him softer than us. I'm glad he didn't follow in our footsteps and enter the criminal bar, aren't you?'

Jim nodded. 'But it doesn't mean I'm not proud of what you've achieved. I just wouldn't want anyone else I love to have to shoulder the burdens that we do. We carry the knowledge of all the murderers who we've helped to walk free over the years - and the ones who haven't.'

Sally put down the glass and adopted a serious expression. 'You've never brooded on this stuff before. It's part of the job and we accept it. I learnt that lesson from *you*, Dad.'

'I know. But this time it's different. I'm not quite sure why, but it is.'

Chapter 19

Despite it being a Saturday morning, the Clyde Valley University Library was busy. But then it was the middle of term for its students, Dani noted. Rhodri had organised for her to have the use of a visitors' pass. The archive service had been informed of the information she was interested in accessing, so it was ready when she arrived.

It wasn't long before the DCI was comfortably positioned at a corner table, flanked by windows overlooking the campus, with all the relevant material laid out in a couple of neat piles on its glossy surface.

Most of the print-outs were copies of articles originally published in the Glasgow Herald. There were dozens of them, the first dating back to February 1972.

Dani examined the photograph of Heather Conlon, the first victim. Her hair was thick, curly and dark. Although the shot was black and white, Dani could tell that her thin lips were painted a deep red and her lashes accentuated with mascara. Heather was 19 years old when she went missing, the youngest of the victims.

This short article outlined the last time Heather had been seen by her parents. She'd lived at home with them in a quiet suburban street in Kilmarnock. Heather was a trainee stylist at a local hair salon.

The girl had gone for drinks at a pub in the centre of town with some workmates. She'd left at quarter to eleven, saying she'd catch the bus home, but never got there. Local police were appealing for witnesses. There was a contact number given at the foot of the page.

Dani considered how revolutionary CCTV was to her job as a detective. If Heather went missing nowadays, there would at least be grainy pictures of her in the town centre. They would know if she ever reached the bus stop and certainly if she actually travelled on the bus itself. In the early seventies there was nothing. Without witnesses, the girl was pretty much untraceable.

The next time Heather Conlon was mentioned in the papers was when her case was linked to the subsequent disappearances of Cheryl Moss in the summer of 1972, then Kirsty Glendinning in April '73 and finally Debbie Cane, in the August of 1974.

Dani looked at each of their photos carefully. The young women were all slim, dark haired and pretty. Their features were small and neat. There was a wholesome appearance to each of these girls, even if a couple of them were known for having strings of boyfriends; sometimes seeing several men at the same time.

Cheryl Moss and Kirsty Glendinning were the oldest of the victims, although neither was more than 25 years of age. These two were the ones who were regulars on their local pub and nightclub scenes. They had numerous gentlemen companions and occasionally left the clubs with men they'd only met that night. Dani knew all this from the police reports.

These two women were what Dani and her team would now identify as having lifestyles which made them category 'A' targets for a serial sexual offender. Heather Conlon and Debbie Cane were younger, lived with their parents and were taken by the killer whilst enjoying a rare evening out.

Because of the differences in the four women's profiles, Dani would have concluded that the killer was an opportunist. He preyed upon certain areas and venues rather than specific individuals. She wondered if DCI Harry Paton had come to the same conclusion. Dani thought he must have done, because the taxi driver theory fitted with that scenario very well.

Dani took out her pad and made some notes. Something about the dates of the murders was bothering her. There was a seven month gap between murders one and two, then a nine month gap between two and three.

But the third girl, Kirsty Glendinning, went missing in the April of 1973 and the fourth not until the August of 1974 – a gap of a year and four months. This was a much larger break than there had been with the earlier cases. It didn't match the established behaviour pattern of the killer.

The DCI's phone began to buzz in her pocket. She dug it out, noted it was James and decided to return the call when she got outside.

Dani glanced back at the print-outs. She sifted through the pile until alighting on the newspaper accounts of the discovery of the bodies. This story had hit the front pages of the nationals as well as the Glasgow papers.

There were several photographs of the cave, but they didn't show much – just a band of police tape outside the entrance and ashen-looking young officers hanging around smoking cigarettes and sitting on rocks near the shore. So much for the sanctity of the crime scene.

The remainder of the coverage was reserved for Calvin Suter. His humourless face accompanied every single article and by-line relating to the murders. Grisly details of supposed sexual torture and even witchcraft made up the majority of the sensationalist text.

Then Dani found what she was looking for, a relatively fact-based account of what the police discovered in the cave, which was reported in one of the national broadsheets. Only four bodies, all of them female; identified by medical and dental records.

She sat back and sighed, tapping her pen on the desk. Then why the break of over a year? Dani desperately wanted to ask Calvin Suter this question. But something told her that he wouldn't be very keen to answer it.

Chapter 20

Before she returned the documents, Dani had one more thing to check. The final article in the pack related to the disappearance of Sarah Martin. She was the 26 year old from Fenwick who went missing whilst Calvin Suter was in prison.

The family must have supplied a photograph because an image of the young woman was staring out of the front page. Dani caught her breath. Sarah was smiling broadly at the camera, her even features carefully made-up and her wavy dark hair framing a very pretty face.

Sarah Martin was undoubtedly a similar physical type to the other four girls. Dani read the piece carefully. The circumstances of this woman's disappearance were slightly different. Sarah had a secretarial job in the city and commuted home each day. She lived with her partner, Ed Callan, who worked as a steward on the ferry to Belfast. His job was based in Irvine. He'd been away on a voyage when his girlfriend went missing.

Dani tried to read between the lines. It seemed that Sarah had gone out drinking in her local pub alone. She'd been seen there by several witnesses, one who identified her drinking with a man, for at least part of the evening. After 11pm there were no further sightings.

Callan returned to their flat the next day and discovered the bed hadn't been slept in. Sarah Martin didn't turn up at work. No one had set eyes on her since.

The DCI concluded there was another man involved. Sarah had met him that evening, knowing her boyfriend was going to be away overnight. She wondered if the guy was ever traced. He'd have to be their prime suspect. Callan was working on a busy ferry, with umpteen witnesses. The boyfriend would never have been in the frame.

She glanced at her watch and gathered together the papers, moving across to the archive desk to return them. Dani ducked into the toilets to freshen up. She was due to meet James for lunch in quarter of an hour. Dani ran the tap and cupped the warm water in her hands, splashing it over her face and closing her eyes for a moment.

In that instant, the DCI heard one of the cubicle doors behind her squeak open. Before she could rub the water out of her eyes, Dani found herself doubled over the sink, her face shoved down into the tiny pool of water that had gathered in the bowl. She heard the taps being turned on once again. A gush of liquid spilled out onto her head, pooling around her face and submerging her mouth and nose.

Dani wriggled frantically, but the grip on her body only tightened further. By this stage, she couldn't breathe and could feel the water spilling over the top of the basin, wetting her blouse and trousers. When she managed to lift her head a fraction, Dani heard voices. Her attacker jerked backwards, allowing her to wrench her face out of the water and collapse onto the floor, coughing and wheezing for air.

Suddenly, someone had an arm around her. 'Are you alright, Miss?'

'I'm a police officer,' she managed to pant. 'Where did he go?'

'I'm sorry, he barged past me and took off. I wanted to check you were okay before getting security.'

Dani levered herself up.

The girl kneeling beside her was clearly a student.

'Don't worry. It was good of you to challenge him. You were very brave. Could you provide a description?'

The girl smiled. 'Shouldn't you be getting to hospital before you start questioning witnesses?'

Dani dug the phone out of her pocket and began dialling. 'I'm afraid there's no time for that.'

*

As requested, DS Mann had brought a change of clothes for her boss. Dani knew they were roughly the same size and the sweater and jeans fitted perfectly. She emerged from the disabled cubicle, rubbing at her short hair with a towel.

Alice and Andy were dressed informally, but a couple of uniformed PCs, plus the campus security guards, were examining the scene.

'The library and campus are full of CCTV cameras,' Andy declared. 'We'll have plenty of footage of the guy.'

'But nobody's found him yet?'

Alice looked sheepish. 'No, Ma'am.'

Dani sighed. 'It's not your fault. I should have gone after him.'

'We've got the witness statement.'

'Yes, but Grace said he was wearing a cap and kept his head right down as he barged past her. She doesn't know if she would recognise him again.'

Andy put his hand on her shoulder. 'Let's just be glad the girl interrupted him. Do you want me to give James a call?'

'Shit! We were supposed to meet for lunch. That was nearly an hour ago.' Dani delved into the pockets of the jeans, searching for her phone.

'You won't find it there, Ma'am,' Alice said kindly. 'All your stuff's in this evidence bag.'

'Oh, yeah, thanks.' Dani reached out for it.

'Look. I think we should go and get you checked out,' Andy insisted. 'Let me drive you to the Infirmary. *I'll* give James a ring and ask him to meet us there. Okay?'

Dani nodded, allowing Calder to take her by the arm and lead her purposefully towards the main stairs.

Chapter 21

'She wasn't behaving quite right. She was a bit shaky and disorientated, you know?' Andy handed James Irving a coffee from the machine.

'Well it's no bloody surprise is it?' James was taking deep breaths to calm himself down. 'Was this a random attack do you think? Could it be related to a case you're handling?'

Andy shook his head. 'I don't think so. Alice and I are putting the heat on a suspect. We're looking for an unidentified male who may have killed more than once, but the boss isn't really involved in the investigation.' The DC took a sip of his drink. 'What was she doing at the university library in the first place?'

James' expression was grave. 'Dani is looking into an old murder case. Forty years old to be exact. The man convicted of the abduction and murder of four women in the 1970s has recently been released. My father was the one who defended him in court. Dani is interested in it on my account.'

'Could this attack have something to do with that old case, then? Maybe someone followed the boss to the library and got wind of what she was up to.'

James stared down at the cup in his hand, as if the contents were poison. '*Jesus*,' he sighed. 'I bloody well hope not.'

*

'Are you *sure* you're alright?'

'You've asked me that question a dozen times.' Dani managed a smile.

'That's because I don't really believe your answers.' James snuggled up next to her on the sofa. 'Did the doc say you could return to work straight away?'

'He thought I was in mild shock, but physically I'm fine. I wasn't without oxygen for more than a minute or so, although it felt like longer.'

James' body stiffened. 'What the hell was the man doing? Was he trying to kill you?'

Dani slipped her arms around him. 'I actually don't think so. I believe it was a warning. If he wanted to kill me he would have knocked me out on the basin before drowning me. As it was, I remained conscious throughout. He wanted to send me a message.'

'Which was?'

'I suspect he was interrupted before he could deliver it. I'm pretty sure the gist was that I should stop digging into things.'

'The Suter case, you mean?'

Dani nodded, taking a sip of wine.

'But *why*? Do you think it was Calvin Suter himself?' James shifted round to look at her.

Dani shrugged. 'It could have been.'

'The *bastard*.' James sat forward, resting his head in his hands. 'The man's a cold-blooded killer. He should never have been let out. Can't we contact his parole board and tell them about this?'

Dani laid her hand on his back. 'We've got absolutely no proof it was him. Let's wait for the CCTV footage to come in. We might get something more conclusive then.'

James turned round, scooping her up into his arms. 'Promise me that you won't get any more involved in this? Don't do any more investigating. I know you're trying to help my family, but I'd hate you to get hurt again.'

Dani buried her face into his shoulder. 'I know you would. I'll take a step back. I promise.'

Chapter 22

A bunch of flowers stood on Dani's desk. It was a jolly spray of pink roses and cream chrysanthemums. She thought the choice was rather girly. Not something she'd really expect from anyone who knew her well. Anticipating the card to be from James, Dani smiled to herself as she opened it.

The smile faded. They were from the DCS. He was offering her the best of luck in the interview for superintendent the following week. Dani sat in her chair, now eyeing the flowers suspiciously, viewing them suddenly as an awkward encumbrance, something else to clutter up her already cramped workspace.

Andy knocked on the door, entering before being invited to. He dipped his head towards the bouquet. 'Very nice, Ma'am.'

'They're from Dour Douglas.'

Calder narrowed his eyes. 'Tacky as hell.'

Dani laughed. 'Yeah, I thought so too. What's the latest?'

Andy pulled up a chair. 'We've taken a look at the CCTV footage from the library building and had a word with the manager of campus security. The images were really hard to make out, but we've printed them off. The techies are going to brush them up at the lab.' He frowned.

'What is it?'

'The guy was wrapped up in a padded jacket. The cap obscured his face in all the shots. The thing is, he matches the description of a man who's been attacking female students on campus.'

'Why don't we already know about this?'

'The security manager says it's only happened a handful of times in the last few years. In each case, the girl involved didn't want to call in the police.'

'Were the attacks sexual in nature?'

'The security guy thinks so. The students were fairly drunk when they were set upon by this man. In a couple of instances, the girls were headed back to their rooms after a night out in one of the student bars. They kinda felt it was their own fault for being inebriated and leaving themselves vulnerable. I expect that's why they didn't want the police involved.'

'If they'd come to us immediately we could have explained that an assault is *never* the victim's fault.' Dani ran a hand through her hair. 'We need to get these girls to make formal statements. Can you find me the College Principal's number? I'll have to give him a call.'

'Your case doesn't quite fit the pattern. But the man *was* hiding out in the ladies toilets. Maybe after he'd incapacitated you, he was planning to drag you into one of the booths...'

Dani directed a steely look at him. 'In broad daylight? In the middle of a library - with dozens of people milling about?'

'The statements described him as 5'10 to 5'11 inches in height, Caucasian, with a bulky build. This matches the CCTV footage of your attacker perfectly.'

'I don't care, Andy. The attack on me was *not* sexual.'

Calder placed his hands in the air. 'Okay. I'm going to take your word for it, of course. But maybe you should just have a couple more days off. The whole incident was a shock. The doctor said so himself.'

Dani looked down at the papers on her desk. 'I'm fine. Now, can you check in with Phil? Because he really wants you to wind up this garage arson business. Make it a top priority would you?'

Andy stood up. 'Yeah, sure. I'll get straight back on it.'

'Good. Please close the door on your way out. I don't want to be disturbed for a while.'

'Whatever you say, Ma'am.'

*

Andy strolled around the empty lot. The damaged cars had been towed away, leaving a large expanse of concrete, scorched black in several places where the fire had raged. He held the arson report in his hands, deliberately standing on the spot where the blaze had started.

A man in a shabby suit exited the nearby pre-fab and walked towards him. 'Any news yet on the bastard who did it?'

Calder shook his head. 'We've got no prints on the wreckage and an incendiary device made from supermarket fireworks. You're sure there's nobody who's got a grudge against you or the business? It could be a customer, maybe. Someone who felt you'd sold them a turkey?'

The man narrowed his eyes belligerently, before deciding it wasn't worth taking offence. 'I'll ask Val in the office again. She often fields those kinds of calls for me. We offer to fix stuff for free within the first two months of a purchase. There isn't much bad feeling amongst our clients. This is a reputable operation, Detective.'

'Where do you get your vehicles from – have you got any associates who may have made enemies?' Andy felt as if he was clutching at straws.

'I'll give you a list of our suppliers. We've recently

branched out into handling a limited selection of classic cars. Over the past ten years, I'd noticed a growing interest amongst our older businessmen clients. I thought it might be an area we could specialise in.'

Calder was interested. 'Okay, that's new. Were any of these vintage cars damaged in the fire?'

'We had a couple out here on the forecourt, the rest are in a barn on the field out the back. Those cars are fine.' He laughed bitterly. 'That's the only stock I've got left now. Looks like my future might be at the auctions.'

'Give me that list and I can check out your newest suppliers. If you remember anything else that might be important, just give me a call.' Andy handed the man his card.

'Sure, I'll have a word with Val and get back to you.' He slipped the card into his jacket pocket. His expression was devoid of all enthusiasm.

Chapter 23

The plane had touched down at just after 9am. It was a short taxi ride from the airport to the centre of Belfast.

After a stroll through the botanical gardens, Dani led James into a café near the university to grab some early lunch. They took a table by the window.

'What are you planning to do whilst I'm gone?' Dani picked up her cup and slowly sipped the milky cappuccino.

James had a map laid out on the table before him. 'I thought I'd take one of the taxi tours around Shankill Road and the Falls. It seems to be what the tourists do.'

'Aye, it's fascinating. If you find a decent looking restaurant on your travels, book us a table for tonight would you?'

'Sure. I'll check into the hotel too.' James downed his espresso, turning his attention to the sandwich the waiter had just delivered. 'We *will* get a chance to relax – after you've done what you need to?'

'Of course. The DCS gave me a couple of days off to recuperate. He was amazingly sympathetic actually. It almost made me think he wasn't planning to undermine my team whilst I'm away.'

'You were assaulted, Dani. The guy's only human.' James wiped his hands on a napkin. 'When were you last here?'

She furrowed her brow. 'It must have been a decade ago now. Dad and I were in Belfast for a family wedding. I've not seen Marsha and Tim in years. I don't expect I'll see them on this trip, either.'

James leant forward, taking her hand. 'We could,

you know. There's no reason why you have to keep this appointment. You promised to take a step back.'

'I need to. Somebody out there doesn't want me rooting around in past history. I'm going to find out why not.'

*

The taxi took Dani out to Jordanstown, to the east of the city. The address she'd given the driver was down a leafy, pleasant street near to a large park. She got out and closed the door, having told the cabbie to return for her in an hour.

The house was semi-detached and modestly sized. Dani approached the front door and pressed on the bell. A broad man in his sixties opened up. He invited her in with a barely softened Glaswegian accent.

'Mr Callan, I'm very grateful that you agreed to meet with me today.'

Dani followed him into a wide sitting room which looked out onto a garden bordered by a line of tall trees. She imagined this was the boundary of Loughshore Park.

'Sit yourself down, Detective. I'll fetch us a coffee.'

Dani sat obediently on the sofa, taking in the bank of photos on the fireplace. She could make out children at various stages of their lifecycles; at graduations, weddings and christenings. Right now the house felt deadly quiet. There was clearly no one at home but them.

Ed Callan returned with both hands full.

'Thank you,' Dani said.

He handed her a mug and took the armchair. 'So, you want to know about Sarah.'

'Yes please. I realise it was a long time ago. Anything you can recall about her disappearance would be useful.'

Ed's eyes flicked unconsciously towards the photographs. 'My wife doesn't know very much about what happened with Sarah. Our children know nothing at all.'

Dani put up her hand. 'There's no reason for this conversation to be official. I've been reviewing the case histories of young women who went missing in the Kilmarnock area during the 1970s. Sarah Martin's case was an obvious place to start.'

Ed nodded. 'I was away on the boat the night it happened.'

'When had you last seen your girlfriend?' Dani pulled out her notebook.

'It was the morning of the day she disappeared. I had to leave very early to get to the port, but we had breakfast together. Sarah got the bus to Kilmarnock and then the train into Glasgow Central. Her office was in Charing Cross. We spoke briefly before I left. About the weather, as it happens.'

Dani raised her eyebrows, amazed the man could recall this detail.

Ed smiled. 'The conditions were a preoccupation for the boat crew. It was late April, but the Irish Sea could still be very rough. The forecast was for high winds along the west coast, coming down through the Clyde. I was wondering if there might be delays. That's what Sarah and I discussed.'

'And this was a common occurrence, for you to be away overnight with your job?'

He knitted his brow. 'Yes. The police inspector back then made a lot of that. He was convinced Sarah was meeting another man in the pub that night. The truth was that we were both young, had busy jobs and lots of friends. The fact that I worked on the boats was never a big issue between us.'

'When did you discover that Sarah was missing?'

'I called her office from the port in Belfast. There had been some delays and the voyage was choppy, but we got there eventually. I always let Sarah know that I'd arrived safely.' Ed cleared his throat, swiping at his eyes with a beefy hand. 'Sorry. I never expected to get emotional talking about this. It's been *thirty seven* years for heaven's sake.'

'It's fine. Take your time.'

'We only spoke for a few minutes. She said she was going to have an early night. That much I do remember. I said I'd see her the following day, and that I loved her.' Ed's voiced cracked. A large tear escaped onto his cheek.

Dani felt her stomach tighten. She hated having to dredge up these terrible memories for people, especially if it turned out to be for nothing. The DCI sat back and finished her coffee, allowing the man seated before her to compose himself once more. 'But she *did* go out that evening. Was it usual for Sarah to do that, on the nights you were away?'

'I didn't think so, but then I've realised since the whole awful business that you never really know another person, not completely. I trusted her and she trusted me. That in itself should have alerted me to something back then, but it didn't.'

'How do you mean?' Dani looked puzzled.

Ed glanced around him. 'Well, you must have wondered how I ended up here in Belfast?' He sighed heavily. 'I met Bridget Reilly in early '78. She was the sister of one of the guys who crewed on the boat with me. We had dinner at his family's house a few times when we had a stop-over. By the time Sarah disappeared, I was staying at Bridget's place whenever I was in Northern Ireland.'

Dani put down her pen and glanced up. 'Did the investigating team in Kilmarnock know this?'

Ed shook his head. 'They were satisfied that I

was in another country when Sarah was taken. I didn't want to upset her family by telling them everything.'

'It would have made you a suspect and given credence to the theory that your girlfriend was seeing someone else. The SIO would have widened his search, come out to Belfast to check your alibi more closely, to see if you couldn't have taken an earlier boat back to Scotland.' Dani eyed him carefully.

'You could still ask those questions now. Bridget saw me off on the boat that morning - the 24th April 1978. I got into shore exactly when I told the police.'

'Did you go straight to the flat in Fenwick?'

'Yes. The place looked eerily like I'd left it twenty four hours earlier. I rang Sarah's office and they told me she'd not come in. I called her parents and some of her girlfriends. It didn't take me long to inform the police. It was totally out of character.'

'Might Sarah have found out about your relationship with Bridget? It may have encouraged her to leave you that day, with another man perhaps?'

Ed ran a hand through his thick, grey hair. 'Aye, I certainly considered it, but not for very long. Sarah's not been in touch with her sister or her parents whilst they were still alive. Whatever *I'd* done, she'd not have cut herself off from them. The family were always close.'

Dani leant forward. 'Why were you carrying on this secret life here? Why hadn't you just told Sarah that you'd met someone else?'

Ed rubbed hard at his face, as if trying to remove a stain. 'Because I loved her. Between you, me and these four walls, I don't know if I'd have married Bridget if Sarah hadn't disappeared that night. I was undecided back then. With Sarah gone, the relationship with Bridget strengthened and grew. I needed her to help me through it. I was a bloody mess for months. We married in 1980. The kids came along soon after. I've got grandchildren now. But don't imagine I don't see Sarah's face in my head every single day, because I do. She was so pretty, a bit like a young Liz Taylor, I always thought.' Tears were coursing down the man's face. 'I wasn't there to protect Sarah, like she deserved. I hope you find out what happened to her, Detective. Please don't give up looking like the last lot did. The answer must surely be out there somewhere.'

Dani gripped his hand tightly. 'I'll do the very best I can, sir. I promise.'

Chapter 24

Dani hadn't said much throughout dinner. She let James do all the talking, about his tour of the Shankill Road and the Victorian architecture of the city.

'You know, the place actually reminds me a lot of Edinburgh,' he continued, pouring more wine into their glasses.

'But that ever present legacy of *the troubles* reminds me more of Glasgow,' his companion put in, sipping the Merlot with relish.

'Ah, so you *have* been listening.' James grinned.

'Of course, darling.' Dani smiled back. 'I've just been thinking about Ed Callan and Sarah Martin, that's all.'

'I know. I've been thinking about them too. It's very sad. You wonder what would have happened to the couple if the poor girl hadn't been taken. They may have been the ones to get hitched and have kids and grandkids. There's a whole alternative history there that never got the chance to be played out.'

Dani gripped her wine glass. 'I think Ed was overplaying things a little. In the wedding picture of him and Bridget they looked very much in love. I get the feeling he would have broken things off with Sarah eventually, which doesn't make her disappearance any less heart-breaking. There was still a life for her she never got to live.'

'Could Callan have come back that morning, on the 24th April, and killed Sarah? Say he found out she'd spent the night with another man? Just because *he* was being unfaithful, it doesn't mean the guy would be happy for her to do the same.'

Dani shook her head. 'There wasn't time. I checked the investigation files again. It took Callan just over an hour from reaching the flat in Fenwick to calling the local police station to report Sarah missing. That wouldn't have given him the opportunity to do anything, let alone dispose of a woman's body so that it was completely untraceable for forty years.'

'So the man she was seen with at the bar on the evening of the 23rd is the most likely suspect? How on earth can you identify him now – after all these years have passed?'

'Well, I can't. I know I made a promise to Ed, but without a body we've got nothing. I'll go back over the witness statements again. I'm not really sure what else I can possibly do.'

*

Alice Mann turned the screen round so that Calder could view the image. 'Here, at 1.47pm, the camera at the junction on the Great Western Road, near to St George's Cross, caught a car jumping the red light.'

Calder squinted. 'It's a Ford Fiesta, I think. Looks black in colour. Can you read the plates? What do the traffic people have to say?'

'The department were still processing the information. They were generating an official letter when I spoke to them.'

'Does that mean they have an address?' Andy glanced hopefully at his colleague.

She smiled broadly. 'Yep, it certainly does.'

He grabbed his jacket. 'Then what are we waiting for?'

*

The house wasn't exactly what Andy had been

expecting. It was an impressive Victorian villa, set within a row of identical properties on the outskirts of Maryhill. They were deep into middle class territory.

As Alice pulled up onto the drive they saw the black hatchback, parked in front of the garage. Andy got out first, proceeding to walk around the vehicle, carefully inspecting the paintwork on the front bumpers.

He waved Alice over. 'The car is almost brand new, but look,' he pointed to a scuff beneath the light on the driver's side. 'There's a dent in the panel here, too. You can only spot it when the light shines on the surface a certain way.'

Alice nodded. 'I see it.'

The officers glanced up as the front door opened. A thin woman in her fifties stepped out. 'What do you think you're doing?' She called down.

Alice pulled out her warrant card. 'My name is DS Mann and this is DC Calder. We're from the Serious Crime Division. May we come in and speak with you, Mrs Tulloch?'

The woman's belligerent posture sagged slightly. 'Yes, of course.'

The interior was beautifully decorated, but Andy found it sterile. The units and worktops which lined the impressive kitchen were all a glossy white. It actually reminded Calder of the sealed room where Dr Culdrew cut up his bodies at the morgue.

'Are you Mrs Glenda Tulloch?' Alice took a seat at the breakfast bar.

'Yes,' the woman replied tartly. She remained standing.

'And you are the registered keeper of the vehicle parked outside on the driveway?' Andy continued.

She nodded. 'The Fiesta is mine, yes. I drive it to work.'

'Where do you work, Mrs Tulloch?'

'I'm a receptionist at the Fitzroy Art Museum, near Kelvingrove Park. I do three mornings a week. Monday, Tuesday and Wednesday.'

'Does anyone else have access to your vehicle?' Andy subjected the woman to his steeliest gaze.

Glenda Tulloch blinked rapidly. 'My husband, of course. But he mostly drives the BMW. He finds my car too cramped inside.'

'Anyone else,' Alice persisted. 'Your children perhaps?' DS Mann made a point of taking out her pad and flicking through it. 'Matthew Tulloch aged 28, or Francesca Tulloch, aged 23?'

'We didn't add the children to the insurance policy. The premium was far too high. Matt and Fran both have cars of their own. They don't need to use mine.' Glenda put a hand up to her neck. 'What is this about? Have I been caught speeding?'

'Where were you on Wednesday afternoon of last week, at between 1.30 and 2pm?'

Calder felt as if he could almost hear the mechanisms in her brain whirring.

'I don't want to answer any more questions without my husband and lawyer present.'

'That is your right, of course. We only wish to get a few simple matters cleared up.'

'Until you tell me exactly what those *matters* are, Detective, I'm not saying another word.'

Chapter 25

DCS Douglas rested his weight on the edge of Phil's desk, appearing to mull the request over carefully. 'I suppose you don't know who Brian Tulloch is?' He finally asked.

Alice shook her head. 'Should I, sir?'

'He's the chairman of the Glasgow Business Re-Development Council. I've met him at a few dinners.'

Andy Calder bristled. He was determined to say nothing. Douglas didn't like him. Alice was the golden girl. He was leaving this all up to her.

'That shouldn't make a difference, surely? Mrs Tulloch's car was very likely involved in a hit and run which left a grandmother dead.'

'And you think it wasn't Mrs Tulloch driving the car? What do the CCTV images show?'

'They're too grainy to tell. The car is all that can be identified with any certainty. Glenda Tulloch is refusing to give us anything unless there's a lawyer present. We need to make this official, sir. We'd like you to hand the Kerr case back to this department. The connection between Kath Nevin's death and the Kerrs' suicides is just too strong to ignore.' Alice held her breath, unsure if she'd gone too far.

The DCS rubbed his chin. 'This decision isn't going to be popular, but go ahead, bring Mrs Tulloch in.' Douglas raised his index finger menacingly. 'Make certain you've done your homework first. See if you can find a link between the Tullochs and either the Kerrs *or* Lisa Abbot. I'm going to get an earful from upstairs on this, so the results had better be bloody good.'

Alice smiled eagerly. 'Of course, sir. Thank you.'

'We need to work fast,' Andy said, slipping into the seat opposite Alice. 'Glenda Tulloch could be getting her car fixed as we speak. I wish I'd never gone over to look at it, we only alerted her to any damage that might have been there. If she wasn't the one driving on the day of the hit and run she may not have previously been aware there was any evidence to get rid of.'

'Don't dwell on it. We would have needed a warrant to seize the car anyway. Let's see what we can find on the Tullochs. The hit and run is only part of the story.'

'Tell that to Kath Nevin's daughter and grandson,' Andy muttered under his breath, but he fired up his laptop and started work, in the full knowledge that Alice didn't deserve his crankiness. 'I'll take Mr and Mrs, you look into the kids.'

After an hour, Alice moved over to the coffee machine to fix them both a drink. When she returned, Andy's vision was still glued to the screen.

'What have you got?' She perched beside him, sipping from her Stirling University alumni mug.

'Mrs Tulloch is just one offence away from losing her driving licence.'

'*Really*? What did she get her points for?'

'Speeding on the M8 mostly. One time, she was clocked at over 100 mph.' Andy sat back and lifted his drink.

'She didn't look the type.'

'No, I don't believe she is.'

'How do you mean?'

'Well, the last time the lady was captured by a speed camera was at Junction 18, not far from where the same car jumped the red-light on Great

Western Avenue.'

'Glenda does drive into the west-end for work. She could have been returning home from the gallery.'

'At half past two in the morning?' Andy swivelled the screen round so she could see.

'Ah, I get your drift. Our Glenda didn't exactly look like the kind of person who races her car in the middle of the night. So, are we thinking that she's quite used to taking the rap for another member of her family?'

'Absolutely. The only question that remains is which one?'

Alice put down her cup and picked up a pad. 'Matthew Tulloch is 28 years old. He is a director of one of his dad's businesses. The company hire out luxury yachts and cruisers from a marina in Tighnabruaich.'

'Does he live out that way?'

'Yes. He's got a flat in the town. A Mazda sports car is registered in his name.'

Andy knitted his brow. 'It doesn't sound like he needs to borrow his Ma's little hatchback.'

'True. The middle child is Francesca, just turned 23 years old. She graduated from college with a fashion degree last year and now lives at home with mum and dad.'

'She sounds like a much more likely candidate for our clandestine speeder.'

'But Francesca's got a Mini Cooper. There are no offences listed against her licence, which she's held for four years. I don't quite get why she would reserve her irresponsible driving for mum's car. The youngest daughter, Ellie, is only thirteen. She attends a private school in the city and gets a lift there and back with a friend's mum.'

'It doesn't quite add up.' Andy glanced back at

his computer. 'The illustrious Brian also has some points for speeding, but not as many as his missus. One time he was stopped for a DUI, but received a warning, no charge. Looks like the DCS isn't Mr Tulloch's only pal on the force.'

'To be fair, DCS Douglas has given us permission to interview Mrs Tulloch, plenty of the bosses upstairs would have shut the thing down completely.'

Andy grunted a concession. 'Let's try and find a connection with Abbot and the Kerrs, then I say we take full advantage of Douglas's momentary weakness and bring the woman in.'

Chapter 26

It was mid-afternoon when Dani and James arrived back in Glasgow. The DCI decided to go into the office for a couple of hours, despite having been given these few days off.

James was going to go home and put a wash on, get some food in for dinner and have it ready for when she returned. Dani was actually beginning to recognise the benefits of this whole sharing your life with another person business.

Andy and Alice were occupying the same workstation. Both had their heads down. Dani wasn't inclined to interrupt them. She swept straight past and slipped into her office. The first sight that greeted her was the bunch of wilted pink and cream flowers on her desk. She immediately picked them up and dropped them into the litter bin, the card and bow still attached.

Dani noticed a fresh file lying on the top of her in-tray. She picked it up and flicked through the contents. It was the Clyde Valley University report into the attacks on three of its female students that she'd requested from the Principal. He'd been very efficient in getting it to her. If only they'd been so keen to report the assaults to the police in the first place.

The girls' descriptions of the man were pretty much as Andy had said. It was fairly clear that the same perpetrator was involved in each instance. The last time anyone was grabbed by this person was during the previous term, at the end of May.

Dani was still certain that the man who held her head under the water in the ladies toilet was not the same person who attacked these students. The M.O. was completely different. The girls described having a hand placed over their mouths before they were dragged towards a dark and secluded part of the campus. Despite them all being inebriated, they'd managed to wriggle free enough to call out or catch the attention of a passer-by. Whenever this happened, the man released his hold and ran off into the night.

The campus attacker was an opportunist, waiting for his prey to stumble out of the college bars, hoping he'd be able to pull her into the undergrowth unseen, so that a sexual assault could be committed.

Dani looked up from the page with a jolt. Something about this M.O rang a bell. It was remarkably similar to the method employed by Suter, when he snatched those women in the 1970s, from outside the pubs of Kilmarnock. *He* was an opportunist, not targeting the girls themselves but the places where he might procure them.

Dani shook this thought out of her head. She'd clearly been spending too long recently obsessing over the old case. She focused her mind instead, on how she was herself attacked in the library toilets.

The man was rough and determined, but he was relatively calm. When victims of a sexual assault recounted their ordeal, they tended to point out how pumped up and edgy their attacker was.

These men were full of suppressed sexual energy, only gaining a release from the unbearable tension through performing the sexual act itself. The perps were usually desperate to commit the assault, dragging their victims towards a quiet, secluded spot as quickly as possible, so that they wouldn't be disturbed.

In Dani's case, she'd just not sensed that frantic

quality to the crime. It was a violent assault, pure and simple - designed to frighten her, to prevent her from investigating any further. To Dani's surprise, when she put her hand up to her face, her cheeks were damp. Tears had leaked from her eyes without her even noticing.

She'd just managed to scramble for a tissue when there was a loud knock at the door. Dani hadn't invited anyone to enter when DCS Douglas strode straight in. 'Oh, sir. I wasn't expecting you. Did we have a meeting?'

'No.' The DCS looked at her intently. 'I was in the department and noticed the light was on in the office. I didn't think you were back until tomorrow.'

'The flight got in at noon. I wanted to check on something here before the morning.' Dani blew her nose, dabbing at her face in the process.

'You need to be fighting fit for the interview this week, Danielle. There's nothing to be gained by returning too soon.'

Dani noticed the man's gaze drop down to the litter bin by her feet, where the sad looking bouquet had been unceremoniously dumped. 'I'm afraid I didn't get a chance to take them home the other day. When I got in just now, the blooms were well past their best...'

'It's not important,' he snapped. 'If you *are* back in the saddle, then please get your team reined in. DS Mann and DC Calder have been digging around into the Kerr case, despite my direct order that it be transferred to Maryhill.'

'Ah -'

Douglas put up a hand. 'They're actually making decent progress. I've given them back the investigation. But it's broadening out to include some individuals who are very influential in this city. I'm not against that, *per se*, but they need a senior officer watching over them, making sure the department aren't needlessly stepping on any toes. You get my drift?'

Dani stood up. 'Yes I do. And I appreciate you handing the case back to them. I'll make sure the investigation is conducted sensitively from this point on.'

Douglas dipped his head. 'Good. Come and see me in the morning, nice and early. We can have a proper de-brief then.'

Dani smiled, bending down to lift the bouquet out of the bin. 'I'm heading back home now. I actually think that with a bit of water and some TLC, I may be able to revive these flowers. It's worth a try.'

The DCS lingered awkwardly for a moment. 'Do whatever you see fit, Detective Chief Inspector. I'll expect you first thing.' He turned on his heels and left.

Chapter 27

Despite the strength of the late autumn rays filtering through the branches of the trees, it was still cold.

Professor Morgan pulled his overcoat tightly around his body as they walked along the woodland path. Calvin Suter had on an expensive looking padded jacket, which bore the name of an exclusive outward bound brand on the shoulder. He seemed entirely unaffected by the chill.

'You're settling well into the new flat?' Rhodri glanced across at his companion.

Calvin smiled. 'Yes, it's perfectly cosy and comfortable. I didn't know very much about Mauchline before I viewed the property, except that the Robert Burns memorial is situated there. Actually, it's very pleasant.'

'And your new place is on the Kilmarnock Road?' Morgan made the inquiry sound as innocent as possible.

'I have moved back to the area of Scotland that I know best, Professor. Am I not permitted to return to my home even after forty years of banishment?'

Morgan could see that Calvin wasn't really offended by the question. 'Not at all. I simply thought that after the release you'd want to get as far away as possible from your past. In fact, I believe it's not such a bad idea to surround yourself with what you find familiar. Too many of my patients seek a life completely at odds with the one they lived before their imprisonment. It doesn't always make them happy.'

'I enjoy the countryside, but I like to be close to the city. My publishers are based in the west-end and several newspapers have approached me to write pieces for them. The payment came through from my interview for Informing Scotland. That money should tide me over for a while, certainly until I receive my compensation.'

The professor's posture stiffened. 'Is that really likely to happen? Your innocence has never been proved.'

Calvin stared off into the distance, where the gorge shelved down towards the River Ayr. 'I have already spoken with a couple of lawyers. There are a number of reputable firms vying to take on my case.'

'That's because of your high profile and the sums involved if you were to prove the conviction was unsafe.' Morgan sighed. 'Many lives will be affected if you pursue this civil action, not least the families of the girls who were killed. Any money you gain will very likely come from the public purse.'

Calvin stopped walking, turning to address his friend. 'How can anyone even put a price on forty years of a man's life? Those were the decades when I would have got married, had children and built a career for myself. I may have gone back to study and taken a degree, without paying the terrible cost of losing my liberty.'

Morgan wondered if Calvin would really have done any of those things. Without the education and guidance he received in prison, the professor strongly suspected that he would simply have gone on to kill more innocent young women.

'The problem Rhodri, is that in your heart you believe I'm guilty. That is why you think I should forget the past and move on. You are probably my only friend in the world yet you still think I'm a monster.' Morgan was about to argue against this point but Calvin raised his hand. 'Oh, I know you'd never use those words but the essence is much the same. I've come to terms with that, I honestly have.' Calvin beat a fist against his chest. 'But *I* know the truth. I want others to know it too. Someone is going to compensate me for my long imprisonment. I've already got a couple of individuals in mind. Believe me, those people are going to pay a very heavy price for putting Calvin Suter behind bars.'

Chapter 28

Mrs Tulloch was seated in the waiting area by the interview suites. Alice left her there for twenty minutes before emerging from one of the closed doors and inviting her inside.

The woman's solicitor bustled in a few moments later. He was overweight and scruffily dressed. Alice felt the man didn't inspire confidence.

Andy nodded to the odd couple before him and flicked on the tape.

'Mrs Glenda Tulloch,' Alice began. 'We have asked you here today to explain your whereabouts on the afternoon of Wednesday, 6th November 2015.'

'I was at work until 1pm. I am a receptionist at the Fitzroy Art Museum. On that occasion, I had lingered in the staff room to eat a sandwich before driving home. I was back at the house by a quarter past two. At which time, I took the dog for a walk.'

Alice slipped a photograph out of a file and pushed it across the table. 'This is a still taken from the CCTV camera at the junction between The Great Western Road and St Georges Cross. It shows your black hatchback jumping a red light.'

The solicitor pulled the picture towards him. 'You can't see who is driving, Sergeant.'

'No, but Mrs Tulloch has already informed us that she is the registered keeper of the vehicle and nobody else in her family ever drives it.' Alice switched her gaze back to the lady seated in front of her. 'Were you driving your car through these traffic lights at 1.47pm on the 6th November?'

'Yes, I suppose I must have been.'

Alice and Andy weren't expecting this.

'You admit to jumping the red light?' Alice leaned forward.

'That is certainly my car. I don't recall doing so, but I must have. It was a very busy morning at the gallery. I may have been tired and didn't notice that the light was red.'

'Isn't this a matter for the traffic department?' The burly solicitor growled impatiently.

Alice kept her gaze fixed on Glenda Tulloch. The woman's face was immaculately made up. Her expression masked beneath a slick of expensive foundation. 'We have a witness who claims that a small back car, matching the description of your Fiesta, jumped that red light on the afternoon of the 6th, just after running down a Mrs Kathleen Nevin. The vehicle failed to stop, leaving the lady lying seriously injured in the road. Mrs Nevin later died of her injuries.'

Andy watched Glenda closely. She barely even flinched.

The solicitor on the other hand, had gone red in the face. 'You have absolutely no proof that it was my client's car which hit this woman. Did the witness identify Mrs Tulloch at the wheel? Did he or she provide the vehicle's registration number?'

Alice sighed. '*No*, but he saw a car, identical to Mrs Tulloch's, speeding away from the scene of a hit and run, so fast in fact, that it jumped the lights a hundred yards down the road. *That* is the point at which we clocked the registration details.'

The solicitor smiled unpleasantly. 'I'm afraid that you don't have enough evidence to connect these two events. My client will plead guilty to the traffic offence. As far as the hit and run goes, she is entirely innocent.'

Alice looked straight at Glenda. 'Is that right, Mrs Tulloch? *You* were the person driving the car in this photograph?' She tapped on the grainy image.

'Yes, if you say that my car was caught on camera at that particular time and date, I must have been.'

Andy Calder decided to intervene. 'This will mean losing your licence for *at least* a year. How are you going to get to work now, eh? I can't quite imagine you hopping on the bus.'

For the first time, the detectives identified a flicker of emotion from the woman. 'I've pleaded guilty haven't I? Why don't you just get on with charging me? Let's get this terrible business over and bloody done with.'

*

Andy reclined in the chair, placing his hands behind his head. 'I've passed the details onto Traffic. They'll be handling it from now on.'

Alice shook her head. 'Damned lawyers. It's simply common sense that a vehicle jumping a red light a hundred yards away from a hit-and-run was the same vehicle that committed the frigging hit-and-run.'

Andy raised an eyebrow. He'd never seen the young sergeant so riled up before. 'Since when has our justice system been based on common sense?'

Alice cracked a smile. 'Aye, that's true enough. That woman was lying through her perfectly whitened teeth. Did you have any luck finding a connection between Lisa Abbot and the Tullochs?'

'Sorry, there was nothing obvious in the records. Abbot's life has followed a course which is a world apart from that of Brian and Glenda. They're like chalk and cheese.'

'What about the Kerrs?'

Andy shook his head. 'Nothing.'

Alice fell silent for a moment, clearly running through the evidence in her head. 'Did we ever check the insurance details?'

Andy sat up straight. 'For Glenda's car, you mean? No, I don't think we did.'

'Because she mentioned it, remember - when we went to her house? Glenda claimed that Matt and Fran weren't added to the insurance because it was too expensive. Let's just double check that shall we? To be sure we've covered every angle.'

'Aye, I'll get onto her company right now. It's got to be worth one final shot.'

Chapter 29

Dani had prepared a meal. It wasn't anything fancy, just a few chicken breasts in a sauce of white wine and herbs. She was simmering a pan full of rice to accompany it.

James was pouring the drinks, his father and sister seated at the kitchen table looking solemn. He deposited a gin and tonic and a neat whisky in front of their recipients.

'Thank you,' Jim muttered, immediately taking a gulp from the glass.

'Was it that bad?' James slipped into the chair next to his dad.

It was Sally who answered. 'The solicitors asked a great deal of questions. This was just a preliminary deposition, but Suter's team appear to be going into a lot of detail, poking right back into the past.'

Dani carried across the two serving dishes, gesturing for her guests to help themselves. 'Have they called any other witnesses to give evidence?'

'There are the lawyers who assisted in the two appeal cases. Police Scotland have released all of the files on the original investigation. DCI Harry Paton is dead, of course, as is Anthony Alderton. Dad is the one left to carry the can.' Sally knocked back a mouthful of her drink, the action not even taking the gloss off her blood red lips.

'They seemed to have spoken with a couple of members of the original jury,' Jim commented. 'There must be a few of them still alive.'

Dani nodded, reaching over to grab a pad off the worktop. She jotted a few things down. 'They might be trying to establish that the original jury were prejudiced by the media representations of Suter before the trial. Calvin hinted as much when I last spoke to him.'

'Is there any chance you and Rhodri can persuade the man to give this up?' James looked pleadingly at her.

Dani sighed heavily. 'Rhodri would have more influence than me, but he's already tried. Suter is absolutely determined. I think the idea of retribution is what's been keeping him going in prison for the past four decades.'

'Then he'd better be prepared for the fight.' Sally dished up some food for her father. 'I've got an army of top rate investigators digging into Suter's past right now. In fact, it's rather refreshing to be gunning for one of the baddies for a change. Calvin Suter has been enjoying the luxuries of the prison service's equivalent of Buckingham Palace for the last few years. When I send him back inside, he won't be going anywhere so pleasant.'

Not for the first time, Dani noted how careful she must be not to get on the wrong side of Sally Irving-Bryant. 'Can you let me know everything that your team find out?'

'Of course. I'll have Mike send you a duplicate copy of all the info he sends me.'

'Brilliant, thanks. Now, come on, let's eat up. We're going to need all our strength for the battle ahead.'

*

Andy put down the phone and crossed his arms over his chest. 'That was weird.'

Alice flicked her head up. 'In what way?'

'I've just spoken with the Monarch Insurance Head Office in Edinburgh. They received our court order this morning and are sending all the relevant documents over by courier this afternoon. But I asked the woman to read out the car insurance details over the phone, so we would know if it was a waste of time or not.'

'*And?*'

'Glenda Tulloch is the main policy holder for the black Fiesta, but there are two other named drivers. The first of them is Brian Tulloch and the other is a 32 year old woman by the name of Sara White.'

Chapter 30

Present at the de-brief meeting in DCS Douglas's office were DCI Bevan, Alice and Andy. The female sergeant was doing most of the talking.

'Sara White was the name that Lisa Abbot used with her married lover, Nick McKenna. We assumed it was purely an alias and never gave it much thought at the time.'

'But Abbot has taken out insurance policies and bank accounts in the name of Sara White?' Douglas eyed his officers carefully.

'Yes. In fact, Andy and I have discovered that Sara White is the woman's real name.' Alice looked sheepish. 'We never thought to check her birth records. Sara White was born at the Glasgow Infirmary in 1983. Her mum was a teacher back then and her dad a carpenter. Sara changed her name by deed poll to Lisa Abbot in 2004. But it seems that she kept certain documentation in both names, a passport, for example, which she has used as identification to secure bank loans and insurance policies.'

'I suppose it makes sense,' Dani put in. 'Fraudsters usually operate under a number of different aliases. We should have looked into the name McKenna provided us with more closely.'

DCS Douglas pursed his lips. 'We couldn't pin anything serious on Abbot then. I encouraged you to scale back the investigation. Now that Mrs Nevin is dead, it's a different matter. What is the connection between Sara White and the Tullochs - why would Glenda put the woman on her car insurance?'

'We don't know yet, sir. But we will need to speak

with Mrs Tulloch again, with your permission of course.' Andy tried to sound as reasonable as possible.

'I'll have to talk to the DCC. This has the potential to become a diplomatic nightmare. Keep digging into the link between this con-woman and the Tullochs and get Lisa Abbot in again for questioning. It seems like she could have been the one driving the car that knocked down Mrs Nevin. Hold off on speaking with Glenda Tulloch until I give you the word.' He switched his gaze to Dani. 'And from now on, I want you present at every stage of the investigation, DCI Bevan. I'm relying on you to be my eyes and ears out there.'

*

Alice Mann laid out every piece of paper relating to the case on the workstation. 'I'll create two piles – one for Lisa Abbot and another for Sara White.' She gazed at the material for several moments. 'It's as if the woman was living parallel lives.'

'Who is to say Lisa had only two identities? She could have possessed many more.' Dani sighed. 'The photographs on Abbot's mantelpiece showed her at various stages of life. At one point, I'd say a decade or so back, she was arm-in-arm with a guy – dark haired and beefy, although I couldn't quite see his face. They were both deeply tanned, almost like they were living somewhere hot.'

'Which could explain the skin cancer,' Andy added.

'I spoke to Abbot this morning,' Alice continued. 'She refused to be questioned without a lawyer. Abbot also said that we couldn't stop her going to the US for treatment. She'd get a court order if necessary.'

'The woman is perfectly correct. We haven't got enough evidence to detain her in the country. Her doctors may very well veto a police interview too. When does Abbot plan to leave?'

'At the end of the month,' Alice replied.

'Then we need to have gathered enough material by that time to be able to stop her.'

'I say we focus on the Tullochs.' Andy got to his feet. 'I've got a yen to check out the kids.'

'Fine, I'll come with you. We need to tread extremely carefully,' Dani advised. 'This family are in thick with the top brass.'

'These people always are, Ma'am.'

Chapter 31

They'd waited until Francesca Tulloch had exited the refurbished warehouse premises on Wallace Street which belonged to the fashion design company she worked for.

Dani yanked the handle of the passenger door. 'I'm going to go in and have a word with the owner. You follow the girl and see where she goes.'

The lobby was minimalistic and achingly trendy. Dani noted the exposed brick walls and concrete floors. The reception desk appeared to have been hacked straight from a fallen tree, with only the barest of attempts made to smooth or treat its oval surface.

'Can I help you?' A woman was shuffling through a pile of papers behind the desk. She was thin, with short blond hair and thick dark liner around her eyes. Dani placed her at maybe forty years old, trying to look early thirties.

She took out her warrant card. 'I need to ask you some questions. Angela Clarke, isn't it?'

The woman stepped forward, putting out her hand. 'Angie. What's the problem, Detective Chief Inspector?'

Dani glanced around the place. There were a few people milling about in a studio on the mezzanine level above. 'It would be better if we could speak in private.'

Angie led the way to a sitting area beyond a glass partition. It contained a sofa and chairs along with a coffee machine. 'This is the closest thing we'll get to privacy here. It's all open-plan.'

Dani tried to place the woman's clipped accent,

deciding it was south of England, perhaps.

'Can I get you a coffee?'

'That won't be necessary, thanks.' Dani sat down. 'How long have you been based here?'

'I moved the business to these premises two years ago. Before that I was selling purely online. I used a lock-up near my flat to store the stock and my front room to do the mail-order. As the orders grew, I knew it was time to do things on a larger scale.'

'That's very impressive.'

Angie smiled warily. 'This isn't about my business is it? I've recently brought in a financial advisor to handle all my tax and stuff. Don't tell me he's been up to anything illegal. I always thought the guy was a bit too slick.'

Dani shook her head. 'Not at all. I wanted to ask you a few questions about Francesca Tulloch, that's all.'

'Fran?'

'Yes. She's worked here for the last six months, is that correct?'

Angie perched on the arm of the sofa. 'Sure, that sounds about right. It was around May time that I received her CV.'

'What are Francesca's duties here?'

'Well, Fran's a Fashion graduate from the Uni. I'm kind of training her up, so she does some design work for me on the new collections. She also does some modelling. To be honest, the girl is brilliant with my digital marketing, which isn't what I brought her in for. I might engage her permanently on our social media platforms. But I've not broached it with her yet.'

'What kind of young lady would you say Francesca was – is she a partier? Lots of boyfriends?'

Angie screwed up her face. '*Christ*, I'm glad no

one asked those questions about me when *I* was 23 years old. It would have been a resounding 'yes' to all the above – the classic profile of a privileged south London party girl. Fran is quite the opposite. She drives her car straight here in the morning and then drives straight home later. The girl still lives with her mum and dad.'

'How do you know she goes straight home after work?'

'Because the rest of us tend to go for a drink on Thursday or Friday evenings. There are a couple of decent bars near here. We all have flats in the city and get the subway or cycle home. I've suggested that Fran get the bus in one day so she can join us. I've offered to pay her cab fare home. But she's not taken me up on it.' Angie shrugged her shoulders. 'Young people are pretty sensible these days, aren't they?'

'Yes, most of them are. It's something to do with the recession, I'm told.'

Angie laughed. 'Yeah, too true. Not like London in the nineties. That was like Sodom and Gomorrah!' The woman looked almost wistful. 'She keeps her cards close to her chest does our Fran. I'd never be totally sure what she thought about anything. But then she's clever, wears my clothes very well and is hardworking. Obviously, that's enough to keep me happy.'

'I can see that it would be.' Dani stood up. 'Thank you very much for being so candid.'

'Fran's not in any trouble is she?'

'No, nothing like that. She's just connected to a case we're working on. There's no question of Francesca being a direct part of it.'

'Right, okay then.'

'But if we could keep this conversation just between ourselves I'd be most grateful. We wouldn't want to alarm the girl unnecessarily.'

'Yeah, of course.' Angie furrowed her brow. 'We certainly wouldn't want to do that.'

*

Dani stood at the end of the road for twenty more minutes, watching the sun set over the river before Andy brought the car to a standstill at the kerb beside her.

'Where did she go?' Dani pulled the door shut, grateful for the warmth being pumped out of the heater.

'Francesca Tulloch went directly to the underground carpark, emerged five minutes later in her car and proceeded to drive straight home to Maryhill, stopping at every red light and staying within the speed limit for the entire journey.'

'Yeah, that's what her boss said she'd do.'

'I waited outside the house for a while. She didn't come out again. I could see lights on in the living room. It looked like Glenda and the girls were settling in for the evening.'

'The other daughter is thirteen, right? There's no chance she could be driving around Glasgow knocking people over?'

'No. From what I could see, the lassie didn't seem the type. Unless pink fluffy onesies are now the required dress code for joy riding.'

Dani chuckled. 'I'd say the girls are in the clear. It might be time to turn our attention to the Tulloch men. We've not heard much from them yet. Let's be sociable and introduce ourselves properly.'

Andy slammed the car into gear, accelerating along the empty street and back towards the city.

Chapter 32

When she was mildly pissed off, Sally Irving-Bryant felt she did some of her best work. As she got older, cases just didn't seem to tug at her emotions in the way they once had. When the case involved her father, it was a different matter.

Sally had demanded her dad go home to their family house in Leith. She had a troop of clerks looking into the background of Aaron Lister. There was no need for Jim to be tiring himself out with that kind of grunt work.

The lawyer ripped open a bulky A4 envelope on her desk and tipped out the photographs and papers. There were a stack of still images showing Calvin Suter's movements over the past week. Sally had him under almost constant surveillance. It was costing her a bloody fortune but what the hell. This was personal.

The man hadn't done a great deal. He'd rented a flat in Mauchline and spent a few days buying items at a nearby homewares store. When Suter drove towards the woods at Ayr Gorge, Mike and his team thought they might be onto something. Perhaps the guy was visiting another dump site. But he'd been meeting Professor Rhodri Morgan for a walk. Suter went straight back to his flat afterwards.

Sally didn't have the authority to tap his phones, or pull his mobile records. She could have asked Dani, but knew it could cost her brother's girlfriend her career to do such a thing. She forced herself to forget it. They'd make do with what they'd got.

Suter had also made a number of trips into the city to meet with his lawyers and a few publishers and newspaper editors. Sally assumed he had a book in the pipeline. She was already onto all of her libel lawyer friends. This bastard would never see his grubby memoirs on the shelves of Smiths. Not as long as she still had breath in her body.

Sally sat back and considered the families of Suter's victims. Why should they have to be greeted with his smug face on a publicity poster whenever they entered a book store or opened a Sunday newspaper? The very idea made her shudder.

In fact, she had all their names and addresses listed there. All the surviving relatives of Heather Conlon, Cheryl Moss, Kirsty Glendinning and Debbie Cane.

This would be Sally's next move, to speak with each of them and gain their support to approach the High Court to press for a gagging order to be placed on Suter. Their endorsement would really strengthen her case with the magistrate.

Sally removed a chunky diamond earing and lifted the phone, deciding there was no time like the present to get the hell started.

*

Dani brought over a tray of coffees and sandwiches. They were seated in the cafeteria of the Business Regeneration Centre in Govan. Brian Tulloch had been in and out of meetings there all morning.

DCS Douglas had supplied them with Tulloch's itinerary for the day, but ordered his officers to under no circumstances make contact with the man.

Andy sipped his drink. 'It makes you wonder why these people work so hard to get a job like this. I'd rather slit my wrists than spend so much time sitting around a glass table listening to management bullshit.'

'I think there's a bit more to it than that.'

Andy slid across the BLT. 'If you say so.'

'But following Tulloch certainly seems to be a waste of our time. Without interviewing the guy, we aren't going to get a damn thing.'

Andy nodded, his mouth full of sandwich.

The phone in Dani's pocket started to bleep. 'Hi Alice, have you got something for us?' She listened for a few moments before ending the call.

Andy raised his eyebrows expectantly.

'Eat up,' Dani said with determination. 'We're going to take a little road trip.'

Chapter 33

The detached house in Irvine was set back from the road, its sweeping drive climbing upwards on a steep gradient. Sally had to floor the gas in her BMW to reach the top and park.

The woman who answered the door was slim and nicely dressed, her ash grey hair worn at shoulder length. Sally knew the owner of the property was in her late fifties and thought she looked well on it.

They walked along a wide corridor into a bright sitting room at the rear. The garden sloped up towards a bank of tall conifers. It appeared to be well tended. Sally accepted the invitation to sit down. Whilst her hostess was busy in the kitchen, the lawyer eyed the photographs on display. The Robertsons gave the impression of being a normal, happy family.

'Here you go Ms Irving-Bryant,' the woman said kindly, setting their cups down on the coffee table.

'Thank you, Jenny. Please call me Sally.'

'I'm very grateful that you came all this way to see me. I know you didn't have to. It's just that nobody has spoken to me about Debbie in as long as I can remember. I really wanted to help you with your efforts.'

'I'm not sure what we can actually achieve. I simply want to prevent Calvin Suter from totally distorting the past and making money out of his crimes.' Sally sipped her tea.

Jenny Robertson sighed. 'I didn't even know he'd been released. I don't always follow the news and my husband wouldn't have told me. He believes we are better off never thinking about what happened to my sister.'

'How old were you when Debbie went missing?'

'I was seventeen. I'd just completed my Highers and was about to go off to College. Of course, that never ended up happening. I had to stay with Mum and Dad.'

'I'm very sorry. Do you remember much about your sister?'

Jenny glanced up, her blue eyes suddenly bright. 'Oh yes. Debbie was lovely, really kind and caring. I'm not just saying that because she died young. She had long dark hair, which was quite thick and a pale complexion. She looked a bit like Snow White - do you know what I mean?'

Sally nodded and smiled.

'Debs never wanted to go to university. She wasn't the academic type like me. My sister had got an admin job in the centre of town and was thinking about renting a flat by herself. Mum and Dad wanted her to get married before she moved away. They were very different times.'

'Did Debbie have a boyfriend in the summer of 1974?'

'I don't think so. The police were very interested in that at the time. Debs had gone out with a boy at the High School when she was still a student there. We knew him really well. But when she left school and got the job I think Debs must have ditched him, because we never saw him again.'

'I don't suppose you remember his name?'

'Oh my goodness, I don't. It's such a long time ago, sorry.'

'But your parents told the police about him?'

'Yes, I'm certain they did. We gave the detectives every piece of information we possibly could. We were frantic to get Debs home.' Jenny blinked wildly, tears pooling in her eyes.

Sally decided the boy's name would be in the police reports she'd requested. This was the type of information that Suter's lawyers would pounce on. They'd want to throw in other potential suspects during any court proceedings, to show that the police were biased to focus purely on Calvin. Sally needed to be one step ahead of them. 'I'll be able to get hold of it then, not to worry.'

Jenny had gulped down some tea and composed herself. 'I know we were lucky, really.'

Sally wrinkled her brow. 'How do you mean?'

'Well, it was only a matter of weeks before Debbie's body was found. She was the last victim. Those other families had to wait years to bury their little girls. I can't even imagine what that must have been like for them.' Jenny broke down. Taking a handkerchief out of her pocket and sobbing into it.

Sally moved across and put her arm around the distraught woman's shoulders. 'I'm dreadfully sorry. I probably shouldn't have come.'

Jenny shook her head violently. 'I've not cried for Debbie in at least twenty years. We've been too busy with children and careers and my parents becoming infirm and then passing away. This is wonderful, actually. I almost feel as if my sister is right here in the room with us. Isn't that extraordinary?'

'How did you all feel when Suter was convicted?' Sally wondered if it was wise to ask this question.

Jenny sat perfectly still, considering her response. 'It was an incredible release. Of course, it wasn't going to bring Debs back to us, but it felt like justice had been done for her, and the other ones. My father, particularly, found it a comfort.' She looked Sally straight in the eye. 'It's hardest for the dads you know. They internalize all those awful feelings of anger, inadequacy and grief. The sentence

Suter received gave my father some peace. It allowed him to carry on, to have a relationship with his grandchildren and claim back something of a life. They don't give out those kinds of sentences any longer. It breaks my heart to think of the victims' families in those cases. To know that Suter was *properly* punished for what he did was so important to us.'

Sally took the woman's hand and gave it a squeeze. For the first time in her long career she'd really heard and understood the perspective of one of the victims of crime. Jenny's speech had affected her profoundly.

Chapter 34

'It's really lovely.' Dani got out of the car and stood at the road side, staring across at the hills and water; a vibrant patchwork of late autumn colours.

'Have you not been to Tighnabruaich before?' Andy asked, coming to join her. 'We had a holiday here once – my Ma, Da and Kathy, I mean. Not Carol and Amy. We took the steamer out to the Kyles of Bute. I loved that.'

'No, I've never been.' The DCI dragged her vision away from the view. 'Now, where does this guy work?'

'Matt Tulloch's business operates out of the marina just beyond the pier. It must be out of season right now. Let's hope we find him there.'

The Tulloch Luxury Cruising offices looked like an upmarket yacht club. Leather sofas lined the reception area. A bank of glass windows revealed the boats themselves, moored along a wooden pontoon.

An attractive young woman smiled broadly as they approached her desk. 'Good afternoon. How can I help you?'

Andy held up his card. 'We'd like to speak with Mr Matthew Tulloch.'

She fluttered her implausibly long lashes. 'Mr Tulloch is on The Princess Louise with a client. I'll just give him a call and inform him you're here.'

Five minutes later, the detectives watched the man stroll along the jetty towards the office. Dani examined his appearance closely.

Matt Tulloch was tall and solidly built. He wore chinos and an open-necked shirt under a cable-knit sweater – posh sailing gear. The man looked older than his twenty eight years, probably because his dark hair was already receding badly.

Dani took a step towards him. 'I'm DCI Bevan from the serious crime unit in Glasgow. Perhaps we could speak in your office?'

A vein under Tulloch's eye flickered ever so slightly. 'Of course, it's this way.'

Dani didn't feel this room afforded them any more privacy. It too was banked with glass.

Tulloch directed them towards a cream leather three-piece suite facing the view. 'Now, what brings you all the way out to Argyll?'

Dani allowed her DC to take the lead.

'There was a traffic incident, sir. It involved your mother, Glenda Tulloch. Her car jumped a red-light on The Great Western Road a week ago.'

Tulloch gave a tight smile. 'That's very unfortunate, but I don't see what it's got to do with me.'

'We believe the same car struck and killed a sixty six year old widow, leaving her for dead at the side of the road. Now, your mother claims to have been driving her car that day, so –'

Tulloch raised his hand. 'Hold on, Detective. You're saying that Mum has admitted to a hit and run on an old lady?'

'Well, she's admitted to the driving offence and we have sworn testimony that the same vehicle committed the hit and run just moments before, so effectively yes, that's what she's done.'

The man shook his head vigorously. 'You must know that Mum would never do such a thing?

'We don't know your mother at all, Mr Tulloch.' Dani shuffled forward in her seat. 'We can only rely upon the evidence, all of which points towards your mother being guilty of causing death by dangerous driving. Now, that's up to fourteen years in prison with an automatic ban. Then there are the points already on her licence. It doesn't bode well. In addition to this, we suspect that the victim was deliberately targeted. In which case, we're looking at a murder charge.'

Beads of sweat had broken out on his brow. 'She's lying. Mum couldn't have been driving that car.'

'How can you be so sure?'

Matt Tulloch sighed deeply and stared up at the ceiling. 'There's another person who drives Mum's car from time to time.'

Andy casually flicked back through his notebook. 'Ms Sara White, you mean?'

Tulloch whipped his head down. 'You already know that?'

Dani directed her steeliest gaze at the man. 'Her name is on the bloody insurance. Who do you think you're dealing with here? A bunch of provincial plod numpties?'

Tulloch went very pale. 'What else do you know?'

'One of our team found out this morning that your family employed an au pair by the name of Sara White from 2000 – 2003. She looked after you and your sister, Francesca. This girl must have become very close to the family to end up being given access to one of your cars, over a *decade* later?'

He nodded. 'We were close, yes. Sara came on holiday with us a few times. She helped Mum out with the house and dinner parties for Dad's clients and politician friends. Our lives were very busy back then. Sara was a Godsend.'

'*So close* that your mother would be prepared to lie for her and risk spending fourteen years in jail?' Dani subjected him to her most incredulous look.

Tulloch wrung his hands. 'I don't know why Mum is lying like this. It doesn't make sense.'

'How old were you when Sara White lived and worked at your house?'

'Erm, about thirteen or fourteen? Fran would have been nine or ten. It was her that Sara was really looking after. My sister probably knew her best out of all of us.'

'What about your dad? How well did *he* know Sara White?'

Tulloch's face contorted with disbelief. 'You can't think that my father had a relationship with the girl. She was only a teenager herself!'

'Sara was nineteen years old when she left your home. She was a fully grown woman. Are you aware that Sara White now calls herself Lisa Abbot? She makes her living by extorting money and favours from people. Sometimes, she will have an affair with one of her victims, later hinting that she'll inform the man's family if he doesn't give her money. But in this case, it's your *mother* who is providing the woman with what she wants. That's why we are confused.'

Tulloch rose to his feet. 'I want to know the name of your superior officer. My father will be outraged to know that you are slandering his reputation in this way. He is a very influential man, with lots of friends in the police force.' Realisation appeared to dawn on him. 'That's why you're talking to *me*, isn't it? Your bosses would never sanction you approaching my father with these crazy theories so you're trying your luck here. Hoping I might be idiot enough to let a nugget of information slip. Well, your little plan didn't quite pay off, did it? I'm going to get straight on the phone to the DCC to report this. Then I'll get Dad's lawyers fully briefed. I cannot believe it's possible to prove my mother was in the car when that lady was knocked down. But I bet you know that too, eh?'

The detectives showed themselves out. Dani

breathed in the fresh sea air before turning to her companion. 'Oh God,' she said. 'I think we're really in the shit this time.'

Chapter 35

Dani was desperately wishing that they were back in the days when DCS Douglas showed no emotion whatsoever. Right at this moment, he was clearly furious.

'You realise that I cannot now sanction the interviewing of any member of the Tulloch household? The DCC is bloody livid. Brian Tulloch is a personal friend of his - Godfather to his daughter, for Christ's sake. *You two* accused the man of knocking off his teenage au pair and taking part in the cover up of the murder of a little old lady.'

'With respect sir, it wasn't quite as blatant as that,' Dani muttered.

Douglas held up his hand. 'I don't want to hear it. This is a cock-up, pure and simple. Certain diplomatic niceties have to be observed alongside the detection in this job. I thought you knew that, DCI Bevan?'

'I do.' To her surprise, hot tears had formed in her eyes. Dani felt the way she did if her father told her off in his wood panelled office at the Colonsay Primary School all those years ago. It was like you'd let someone down twice, as a pupil *and* a daughter.

Douglas's tone softened slightly. 'You can return to the department now DC Calder. Stick to that arson case from now on and liaise closely with Phil this time.'

Dani felt Andy gently nudge her arm as he left. Like a co-conspirator showing their solidarity. It almost made her smile.

'Take a seat Danielle.'

The DCI did as she was told.

'I had a long conversation with the DCC this morning. It didn't all involve him tearing a strip off me.'

Dani raised her head warily. Douglas appeared to be avoiding eye contact.

'I'm afraid that they've decided to remove your name from the shortlist for superintendent.'

'*What*? Because I interviewed a legitimate suspect in a murder inquiry?'

He sighed. 'I want you to know that I did my very best. Once you've moved into the higher ranks, politics becomes as important as policing. You are a wonderful investigator, Danielle. But the DCC doesn't think you are ready to take up a superintendent position just yet.'

Dani got shakily to her feet. 'Thank you for letting me know. May I be dismissed, sir?'

'Of course. Look, take another couple of days off. I don't believe you gave yourself enough time after the assault. Reflect on things and don't be too disheartened. You are young and highly capable. Your opportunity will come again.'

All the DCI could manage was a perfunctory nod of the head before she turned and walked out the door.

*

'I'm so sorry darling.' James placed a glass of wine on the table. He slipped onto the sofa beside her, nuzzling his face into her neck.

'Did I sabotage this thing myself?' She leaned forward and necked the ice cold Sauvignon Blanc.

'Of course not. It sounds like you were really making progress on this case. It's obvious to me that you were getting close to something.'

Dani shifted round. 'And that's why our

investigation got shut down and I lost my promotion?'

'To an impartial observer, I'd say that's how it comes across. Maybe Brian Tulloch makes a habit of bedding young girls. His cronies ensure it doesn't reach the press. It wouldn't be the first time these high-flying types have covered for each other.'

'True. But Lisa Abbot isn't your typical naïve victim. Brian Tulloch must have met his match in her.'

James shifted up. 'This all happened the best part of fifteen years ago, right? Abbot has kept some kind of link with the family ever since. There must be more involved than just the occasional use of Glenda's car. If the woman's got something over the Tullochs then money must also have changed hands.'

'I've got no hope of retrieving their bank records now. Alice was able to find out about Sara White being their au pair because of the electoral register. White gave the Tulloch's Maryhill address when she registered to vote in the 2001 election. She'd just turned 18. That information was of public record.'

'Then you'll have to keep focussing on this Sara/Lisa woman instead. Nobody's sworn you off digging into *her* past, have they? Her path must have crossed again with the Tullochs since 2003. You just need to find out where and for what reason.'

'Well, I'll leave that up to Alice. Andy can't afford to go anywhere near it.' She snuggled into James's shoulder. 'And I'm going to take a holiday.'

James chuckled. 'I'll believe it when I see it.' He sighed. 'Is this new boss of yours really in your corner? Couldn't he have put your case more strongly?'

'Actually, I think he tried his best. I get the feeling that nobody could have changed the DCC's

mind. My chances of ever getting ahead at Pitt Street
have suddenly become very remote.'

Chapter 36

The flat was eerily quiet. James had left for work a couple of hours previously. He liked to get an early start, to avoid the worst of the traffic crawling their way towards the capital.

For the first time in weeks, Dani had a proper chance to think. She filled the coffee machine and nibbled on a croissant that had been left to go hard in a packet. Her head was throbbing mildly. She'd had too much wine the evening before, which wasn't like her at all.

As a result, Dani had experienced some vivid and disturbing dreams. A hooded man, his face always obscured, was lurking along dark alleyways and a few feet away from her in crowds. He was watching the pretty young girls with their arms draped around one another's shoulders, waiting for one of them to be alone, so he could take the opportunity to pounce.

When the phone in the hallway rang, it wrenched Dani away from this unpleasant memory.

'Hello, Dani? It's Sally here.'

'Oh hi. How are things?'

'Fine thanks. James just called me. He told me about the promotion. I'm really very sorry. The management are completely wrong of course. You're a better police officer than the lot of them put together. But since when has that mattered?'

Dani smiled. 'I appreciate your support.'

'James also said you were taking some time off?' The woman's voice was hesitant. 'I'm heading over your way this morning, as it happens. I wondered if we might meet up?'

'Is this to do with the Suter case?'

'Yes, I've been talking to a few witnesses. I'm travelling west to follow up on some new angles.'

'Sure,' Dani replied immediately. 'Just let me know a time and a place. I'll be there.'

*

The café was empty apart from the pair of them. The windows were partially obscured by condensation. Dani could still make out the waves breaking onto the pebbly shore.

Sally looked totally out of place in her designer suit and towering heels seated at a Formica table in this greasy spoon. 'It was Jenny Cane who alerted me to the existence of Johnny Doyle. He was a childhood sweetheart of her sister's. They broke up when Debbie left school.'

'I remember his name being mentioned in the police reports. He left school at this same time as Debbie, going to work as a labourer on a farm down in the Galloway Hills. The police decided it was impossible for him to have got himself from there to Irvine and back on the night she was abducted. Johnny was milking the cows at 5am the following morning.'

'Absolutely, he was eliminated from the enquiries early on. I can easily rebut Suter's lawyers if they put Doyle forward as an alternative suspect.'

'So, much as I love a trip to the seaside, what are we doing in Troon?' Dani sipped her sweet tea, quite happy to take Sally's lead.

'We're visiting relatives.' The woman parted her red lips in a smile. 'Drink up and we can get moving.'

*

The house was down a side street, just off the seafront. Its exterior was a mass of peeling and chipped paint. Dani could sense her companion wrinkling up her nose as she pressed on the bell.

The woman who answered the door was an elderly Afro-Caribbean lady in a flowery dress. 'Can I help you?'

'We spoke on the phone? I'm Sally, from the council?'

The woman stood back, allowing them to enter. 'Have a seat in the living room.'

The interior was dark and cold. Dani imagined that the heating didn't often get switched on. She could see the evidence of damp seeping up through the walls.

Sally pulled a clipboard out of her bag. 'Before we can set a date for the work to be done, Mrs Campbell, I need to take down some details from you.'

Normally, Dani would have had nothing whatever to do with impersonating a council employee. But the way she felt about Police Scotland right now, the DCI didn't much care. Sally was obviously quite used to this kind of thing anyway. She decided to let her get on with it.

'When did you move into this property?'

'I came here with my husband and children in 1983.'

'And where were you before that?'

'In a two-bed flat in Govan. We got allocated this place when my third little one was on the way.'

'How long had you been in Govan?'

The lady sighed, placing her arms across her ample bosom. 'I'd lived around that area since my mother moved to Glasgow from Jamaica. I'm a full British citizen, mind you.' She waggled a finger at them both.

'Of course, that's not in question. You moved into your husband's council property when you got married, is that correct?'

Lena Campbell shifted around in her chair. 'No, *I* was the tenant.'

Sally feigned confusion. 'That's very unusual, for a young single woman to be given a property, when you could have lived at home with your family.'

'It wasn't possible for me to stay at home. The council knew all this. When I turned 18, I was given a flat and I took over looking after my younger sisters.'

'Oh, I see. I think I recall something in your records. The local authority had placed you and your sisters on an 'at risk register'. Is that the reason?'

'This is such a long time ago – can it really be necessary for me to go through it all again now? Just to get my house re-decorated?'

Dani chipped in. 'We have a very long waiting list, Mrs Campbell. Many tenants have young children at home. Their needs are more pressing than yours. If we can ascertain that you have been the victim of a crime and have never received your rightful compensation, we may be able to rush things along a little..?'

Lena squinted her eyes at Dani. 'My mother wasn't a bad woman, but she couldn't cope without having a man about the place.'

'There were boyfriends?'

Lena nodded. 'Lots of them. But one man in particular was the problem. He was called Steve and he wouldn't leave me and my sisters alone. That was in the late sixties sometime. Mum got a job cleaning nights and then it became impossible. I looked after my younger sisters and brother when she went out to work. Steve would show up not long after Mum had left the flat. He made me and my middle sister,

Susie, have sex with him.'

'That's awful. Did you tell anyone?'

'Not when it was just the two of us. When he started on Anna, that's when we told Mum. She was only thirteen.'

'What did your mother do?'

'She told Steve to get lost and changed the locks. But he kept coming round and trying to break the door in. Then we had to bring in the police. The social services got involved and they found out Susie was pregnant. She was fifteen at the time, so Steve got arrested. I think he went to prison. There were more men after him, although the others weren't so bad. As soon as I applied for my own flat I got it. The woman from the council told me it was because they wanted us girls out of that place. Susie and Anna came to live with me for a while, until they got themselves decent fellas. Susie lost the baby, which was a Godsend.'

Dani edged forward on the sofa. 'You mentioned a brother. What happened to him – did he come and live with you too?'

Lena bristled. 'Calvin? He was a lovely little lad when we first came over from Jamaica, full of smiles. Calvin was the lucky one, of course, because Mum's boyfriends weren't interested in him like they were in us. He was okay staying with her, especially when she became too old to attract any more men. Calvin was always the favourite. Isn't that the way with the only boy? Our mum had a soft spot for him.'

'Are you still in contact with your brother and sisters?'

A shadow passed across Lena's face. 'I'm the only one left. Susie and Anna died a few years back and Mum went decades ago. I've got my own kids though, and their children. I see them every Sunday.'

'That's nice,' Dani commented amiably. 'And what about Calvin, are you still in touch with him?'

'Nope. He's dead too, a long while back.' She hugged herself tight. 'Well, he's dead to *me* anyhow.'

Chapter 37

James had lit the open fire in Dani's front room. At first, the logs had smoked badly, the chimney not having been used in years. They were smouldering nicely now. The women sat together on the sofa, an open bottle of wine placed on the table in front of them.

'It was Dad who originally discovered that Calvin Suter had grown up in a house where a convicted child molester had been a regular visitor,' Sally began. 'But Anthony Alderton closed down any further enquiries into Suter's past. With the help of my team, I thought I'd see what I could dig up.'

'You found out that this man's conviction was for assaulting *girls*, not boys.'

'As we all know, these perverts don't stray far from their sick little predilections. I knew there was no way Steve McTierney had abused Calvin, like Dad always thought.'

Dani sipped her wine. 'But he may have witnessed the abuse of his sisters. You heard what Lena Campbell told us today. McTierney raped both her and Susie in that flat. Calvin would have been there the whole time. Being party to something like that can't be very healthy for a young boy's mind.'

Sally shook her head. 'I don't believe he would have known anything about it. Lena was giving into that man's sick demands to *protect* her family. When he turned on one of the little ones, that's when she blew the whistle. There's no way Lena would have allowed Calvin to see what was going on. I bet they went to her mother's bedroom and did whatever they did in there. Calvin was most likely fast asleep through it all.'

Dani was surprised at Sally's insight. She was sure the lawyer was correct. Lena had felt like Calvin was the lucky one, untainted by the horrors of what the others had to endure. He was the favourite, the protected one. 'Then Calvin's got no bloody excuse for what he did to those poor women.'

'No, none at all,' Sally agreed. 'Lena is perfectly aware of that, which is why she refuses to have anything to do with him. Even now he's been released.'

'Rhodri did say that Calvin was estranged from his family. They never visited him once in prison.'

'If somebody close to you is accused of something so monstrous, I suppose you either cling to the belief that the person is innocent, or you disown them altogether,' James added. 'But the family's reaction isn't proof of guilt, we should remember that.'

Dani nodded. 'Of course, but it gives us valuable insights into Calvin's character. This information will be useful when the lawyers come after Jim.'

'Exactly.' Sally leant forward and re-filled her glass. 'Mike is working on finding the surviving jury members. My next move will be to speak with them.'

'Can you afford to be away from your own cases for so long?' James looked genuinely concerned.

Sally's expression hardened. 'This is Dad's reputation we're talking about. I'm hardly going to let a creep like Aaron Lister take precedence over him.'

Dani was surprised. She'd never heard Sally speak about one of her clients in that way before. The detective said nothing, simply rising from her seat and asking if their guest was ready for dinner.

*

Alice Mann was trying to walk a comfortable

distance behind her target, but it wasn't easy. The woman she was tailing had become slow and unsteady on her feet. Alice could see how Lisa Abbot's bulky winter coat was swamping her tiny frame.

Something had made Abbot leave her flat, which she hadn't done in several days. She'd got on a bus and travelled into the city centre. They were now heading towards the St Enoch Centre, where Alice hoped she wouldn't lose her quarry in the bustling crowds.

It was only early November, but the shopping centre had already geared up for Christmas. There were lights and decorated trees everywhere. A plastic Santa's grotto greeted the detective as she entered through the automatic doors.

Abbot headed straight for a coffee shop on the ground level, joining the queue. Alice sat on the bench outside and observed from there. Abbot bought a coffee and proceeded towards a table at the back.

Five minutes later, a man approached the establishment, standing on the threshold and peering inside. When he spotted Abbot, he marched straight in and sat down opposite her, not bothering to queue for a drink.

Alice thought his demeanour was aggressive. He was a well-dressed man whom the detective placed in his early thirties, with dark, receding hair. From the descriptions she'd been given by Andy and the DCI, Alice decided this man was probably Matt Tulloch. In which case, she'd have to keep her distance if she didn't want to lose her job.

The conversation lasted for about ten minutes. Then Tulloch stood up, placing something on the table between them and storming out. He left the same way he had come, blending quickly into the crowds. Alice remained where she was. There was no point in following him.

Lisa Abbot was still at the table, casually finishing her drink. After a few minutes, she reached forward for what appeared to be an envelope. She carefully opened it up and examined the contents. Abbot got to her feet, leaving the coffee shop and heading for the exit.

Alice fell into step behind her, immediately sensing that the woman's stride was just a little bit more robust and confident than it had been when they set out.

Chapter 38

The University Principal's office was significantly larger than his own Professor Morgan noted, but without bitterness. His retirement date wasn't long away and his needs were modest.

'I'm sorry to call you in at such short notice, Rhodri.' Chris MacFarlane shuffled around the papers on his desk. He looked flustered. 'I really need your help with something.'

'Of course, what is it?'

'It hasn't reached the media just yet, thank God, but there was another attack on the campus last night.'

Rhodri sat up straight, his blood running cold. 'Has a student been injured?'

'I'm afraid that a third year girl has been sexually assaulted. She left the student bar at midnight and walked back towards her Halls. A man grabbed her as she emerged from the underpass, dragging her into the bushes.'

'Was she raped?'

The principal's face had gone very pale. 'She's in a terrible state. I'll know more when the police inspector gets back to me. Their doctors are in the process of examining her.'

'At least she's agreed to report it to the authorities. That's something at the very least.'

'She staggered into one of the Porter's Lodges at 1am. They immediately called the police.'

'Good. There shouldn't be seen to be any delays in the university reporting this - as there have been in the past.'

MacFarlane ruffled his greying hair. 'That was

unfortunate. We won't be making such a mistake again. But we rely on our reputation for campus safety to attract future students. We are in a very competitive market place.'

'Nothing is less attractive to people that the whiff of a cover-up, Chris. We are in the centre of Glasgow. There is going to be crime of some description taking place.'

The Principal shuffled up in his seat, making sure their eyes met. 'That's why I wanted to discuss this with you. Do you believe we have a serial offender at work here? What can we do to root out this terrible person?'

Rhodri took a few moments to consider this. 'You'll need to give me access to the reports of each individual case to be sure. From what I already know, this person lurks about the campus at night, waiting for girls to come out of the bars on their own. But the attacks are very sporadic, with sometimes a full year passing before he strikes again.'

'Yes. Apart from the attack on DCI Bevan in the library toilets, we'd not had a case since the last academic year.'

'Then he may not be a student here, or a member of staff. The campus may simply be one of his hunting grounds.'

MacFarlane sighed with obvious relief.

'But he does certainly know the place, so the man must have some kind of connection. I'd say he may be attacking girls in other parts of the city in between times. The police will look into this possibility.'

'What can we do in the meantime to try and keep our students safe?'

'We can't cause panic. The university must carry on with normal life. But girls should be warned not to leave the bars alone for the time being. They should walk in pairs back to their Halls of Residence whenever possible. As staff, we must be vigilant about picking up on any odd behaviour around the grounds and report anything suspicious. Perhaps the police can provide you with an E-Fit image to place about the classrooms and the lecture theatres? Double the number of security guards you have on duty after dark. If this man believes that the campus is no longer an easy target, he may move on elsewhere.'

'Yes, that's good advice, thank you. We need to be seen to take action.' MacFarlane's expression was less strained.

'I'll get in touch with my contacts on the force. Then I can let you know how their investigations are progressing. All I can tell you from my experience as a profiler is that this man will keep offending until he is caught. But these people don't like to take unnecessary risks. They target those places where they've found a blind spot. They are opportunists by nature and are pushed underground if they feel pressured.'

'Then let's pile the pressure on this monster. Let him know he can't get away with terrorizing *my* students.'

Chapter 39

The nurse led Rhodri and Dani towards the hospital room. 'She's a bit groggy because the doctor gave her a sedative. But apart from a few cuts and bruises, she's physically very well.'

'Thank you,' Dani replied, pushing the door open and entering first. 'Hello, Ruth? My name is Detective Chief Inspector Danielle Bevan. How are you feeling?'

The girl was pale and had a purplish bruise on her forehead. 'I'm okay.'

When Rhodri followed along close behind, the girl's face immediately brightened. 'Professor Morgan! Thanks for coming to see me.'

He pulled up chairs for them both. Dani decided it might be best to let the psychologist do the talking.

'How have they been treating you?' He asked gently.

She nodded. 'I've seen a lady police officer and a lady doctor who've been really nice. Do you know if my parents are here yet?'

'They're still on the road I believe. We'll let you know as soon as they arrive.' Rhodri placed his hands in his lap. 'Now, Ruth, I've read through your statement about what happened. I don't want you to recount the whole thing for me again. But I'd like to hear your impressions of this man. Simply try to imagine that we are in one of our criminal profiling workshops at the university.'

A flicker of a smile passed across her young face.

'Tell me anything you can about his build and his clothing. Did you catch a glimpse of his eye or hair colour, perhaps? If you wish to stop at any time, just give me the word.'

Ruth took a deep breath. 'He was tall. I got the feeling that he wasn't all that muscly, although because of his size, it was easy for him to overpower me. His face was stubbly, but the hair wasn't long enough to be a beard. I was pretty drunk but I could tell he'd been drinking too. The alcohol fumes were on his breath. It was beer, I think.' She put up a hand to touch her face. 'When he was telling me to shut up and lie still, I could tell his accent was local and very broad. The type that the students from England claim they can't understand, you know?'

Rhodri nodded. 'I do.'

'His skin was dark but he wasn't black or Asian. The main thing I noticed about him was how jittery he was. It was like he wanted to get it all over and done with as quickly as possible, almost like he didn't want to be there any more than I did which is really weird, isn't it? Then why do it in the first place?' Ruth's voice cracked and a sob forced its way up through her chest.

'It's because they need the release,' Dani explained gently. 'He would have been extremely on edge until he'd done what he set out to do. It's like a compulsion.'

Ruth nodded.

Rhodri handed her a tissue from the box.

'Yes, that's exactly what it was like.'

'Did you get a sense of his age?'

She shrugged her shoulders. 'He definitely wasn't my age, but then he wasn't that old either. I'd say thirties or early forties.'

'And you didn't feel you recognised him?'

Ruth tipped her head to one side. She'd clearly not been asked this question before. 'You mean, had I noticed him hanging around the campus or my Halls of Residence? No, I don't think I did. There was nothing familiar about the man at all.'

The nurse poked her head around the door. 'Ruthie, sweetheart, your parents are here. Do you want me to send them in?'

The girl glanced at her Professor.

Rhodri smiled broadly. 'Of course, we've finished with our questions. It's time to leave this young lady in peace.'

*

They walked in silence back to the car. Dani turned on the engine and said, 'I'll pass that information onto the Serious Sexual Offences team in charge of the case. I know the SIO, she's excellent.'

'When the Principal first told me there'd been an attack, for one awful moment I had the horrible thought that it might have been Calvin, starting up all over again.'

'It's definitely not him. And this guy's a serial rapist, not a sadistic killer.'

'Well, he may turn into one if his crimes escalate. He's already been operating freely for the past couple of years.'

'Yes, he needs to be stopped. Now that the appropriate division are on the case, we've got the best chance we've ever had. Are you going to assist the investigation?'

'They've asked me for a profile, which I'm happy to provide. I can also analyse the locations of his crimes and other reported attacks that followed a similar MO. From this, I will suggest the geographical area in which he is most likely to live.'

'Good. Then they can close in on the bastard.'

Rhodri cleared his throat. 'From what Ruth told us just now, did her attacker sound like the same man who held you down in the ladies toilets at the library?'

Dani gripped the steering wheel hard and continued to stare straight ahead. 'I don't know for sure, Rhodri. I wish I could give a definite answer, but I just can't.'

Chapter 40

Andy Calder shivered as he walked around yet another burnt out car lot, this time not far from Sighthill Cemetery. He wished he'd worn something warmer than his leather jacket. The wind was gusting fiercely from the east.

He noticed a woman in a tight pencil skirt and heels approach him from the main building. She was carrying a cardboard cup. 'Here you go. My boss thought you might appreciate this.'

'Ta very much. Are you his secretary?'

'I'm the receptionist. My name is Kelly.'

'Were you working here on the day the fire was started?'

'Yes, I'm here every weekday. I finished at 6pm and helped Vic to lock up.'

'Did you notice anything unusual – new clients asking too many questions, that kind of thing?'

'As I said to Vic after it happened, the only strange thing was that man who'd come in on the Monday. He wanted to test drive one of our classic cars. He was really well turned out and nicely spoken – not really like our usual clientele! The car he chose to look at, well, it didn't really fit with the sort of man he was. It struck me as weird.'

'Did he buy the car?'

'No. Vic took him out for a spin in it. He said he'd think about coming back for another look. He hasn't been in since.'

'Can I see the car this man was interested in?'

'As a matter of fact you can't. The barn it was housed in was burnt to the ground in the fire.'

Andy narrowed his eyes. 'Let's get out of this

bloody wind. I'll take a proper statement from you and your boss inside in the warm.'

*

Dani was still feeling sombre after her visit to the Infirmary when she met Sally in Royal Exchange Square. The wind was whipping around the buildings in powerful gusts, leaving a trail of fallen leaves in its wake.

Sally wore an ankle length woollen coat and seemed entirely unaffected by the chill. She kissed the detective on both cheeks. 'Do you want to grab a coffee in the Gallery? You look cold.'

Dani followed her friend inside, grateful for the enveloping warmth of the modern cafeteria. 'How's your investigation going?'

Sally's cheeks were flushed with excitement. 'I spoke with *three* of the original jury members yesterday. They were extremely helpful.'

'Do they recall much about the proceedings?'

'Oh yes. They're all retired professionals. The trial of Calvin Suter was one of the most significant events to happen in their lives. They remembered the events very clearly. The important thing is that none of them had taken much notice of the press coverage before the trial. One gentleman was a retired schoolmaster who worked at Wemyss College in the mid-seventies. He claims that the staff common room never held the tabloids. He'd not so much as lifted one up during the furore about the murders.'

'Okay, but that's only one man out of twelve jurors.'

'Yes, but the other two had similar stories. One lady had very small children back then and didn't have time to read the papers. The first thing she'd heard of Suter was when she turned up at the High

Court. The other juror I spoke to was a salesman for a drinks company. He'd been travelling around Europe for the six weeks before the trial.'

Dani sipped her coffee, trying to get the facts straight in her mind. 'If those three are the only jurors left that can be called as witnesses then Suter's team can't claim the first trial was prejudiced by the biased media coverage.'

Sally beamed. 'Spot on!'

'What did they say about the trial itself?' Dani was curious.

'The schoolmaster was absolutely convinced during the trial that Suter was guilty. The fact he led the police to the cave where the bodies were hidden was conclusive to him. He said that Alderton made a good case, but his arguments never cut through that basic fact.'

'What about the others?'

Sally looked less sure of herself. 'The young mum had been very upset by the details of the murders as presented in court. She sensed very strongly that Suter was guilty. I didn't get the feeling the evidence mattered quite so much to her. She was relying on her instincts.'

'And the salesman?'

'He wanted the whole process to be over with quickly so he could get back to work. He was paid largely on commission in those days. But it sounds like he took reasonable notice of the case being put forward. For him, it was Suter's access to the taxi cab seen parked near the places where the girls went missing that swung it. When Cheryl Moss's mother identified the clothes found in the blue Ford Anglia as her daughter's that sealed his guilty verdict.'

'Those pieces of evidence were still purely circumstantial. Did Alderton not make that clear enough to the jury?'

Sally sighed. 'If it were my case, I'd have drilled holes in that evidence so big the entire jury could've walked through it.'

Dani chuckled. 'But was Alderton's performance actually remiss?'

'Not that I can see. Suter didn't receive the best defence in the world but it wasn't negligent. If the jury believes your client is guilty then there is very little that even the most gifted of defence advocates can do about it.'

Dani lifted her half empty cup. 'To the wonderful British justice system!'

Sally tipped her head back and laughed. 'We've got to also remember that no murder case tried four decades ago could ever be conclusively proved. They simply didn't have the forensic technology we do now. There was fingerprinting, sure, but no DNA analysis. We totally rely on that now. To a certain extent, jurors had to simply make an educated guess as to someone's guilt or innocence.'

Dani's expression had become deadly serious. 'We've got those techniques now though haven't we? Tests can be performed on archived samples, even if they're forty years old. Sally, what's happened to all the evidence in this case – like the clothes belonging to Cheryl Moss? More importantly, what became of the car that Suter was supposed to have transported the girls in?'

The lawyer seemed confused. 'Gosh, I've no idea. Surely you're in a better position to find that out than I am? The storage of evidence has got to be a police matter.'

Chapter 41

'Thanks so much for coming over. I didn't fancy going into the department just yet.' Dani stood back to allow her friend to enter.

'Dour Douglas is right, you need to stay away for a bit, have a proper rest,' Andy replied cheerfully.

They headed straight to the kitchen. 'Is it too early for wine?'

'It is for me. Carol's mum is due to come round for tea. I don't want her smelling alcohol on my breath.'

'Fair enough.' Dani filled the kettle instead. 'How's the atmosphere at work?'

'Fine. Once Douglas has given you a bollocking he doesn't seem to hold a grudge. I really think he tried to stand up for you. I bet they never had any intention of giving you the superintendent position. Phil says they've got a DCI on the shortlist from Central Division. He's the DCC's *nephew* for Christ's sake! I reckon they used this Tulloch business to bump you off the list, so it didn't look too much like sexist nepotism when this other guy waltzed into the job.'

'Are you sure you don't want anything stronger?'

Andy chuckled, shaking his head. 'It's always been the same, Ma'am. Bloody office politics. You go ahead.'

Dani poured herself a glass of Sauvignon Blanc. 'I've got an unusual request.'

'Oh aye?'

'I've been looking into an old case involving a client of Rhodri Morgan's. I want to see if I can find where the case evidence was stored.'

'It shouldn't be too difficult, not if you've got the case number. What year was it filed?'

'December 1975.'

Andy nearly spat out his coffee. 'I'm taking it the case was handled by the Strathclyde Police? Otherwise we haven't got a hope in hell.'

'It was. The evidence gathering was done by the Kilmarnock Station but the case was so big all the trial evidence went to Glasgow.'

'Fine, I'll look into it first thing tomorrow.'

Dani took a swig of wine. 'There's a problem, though.'

'You mean other than the fact you're investigating a forty year old cold case when you're supposed to be on holiday?'

'One of the pieces of evidence is a car.'

'A *car*?'

'Yes, there was a private hire mini cab that the defendant was supposed to have used to transport his victims to the place where he raped, tortured and murdered them. I'm hoping there may still be some forensic evidence in it.'

Andy led her over to the table, indicating they should sit down. 'Describe this car to me.'

'It was a 1960s Ford Anglia, they were totally ubiquitous back then, but this one was unusual because of its colour. This was why it got noticed by witnesses near to the spots where the perp picked up his victims.'

'Was it powder blue?'

'I don't know the specific factory colour but it was a light blue, yes. How do you know?'

'Because I took down the description of a powder blue, 1969 Ford Anglia this afternoon. It was destroyed in one of the garage fires I've been investigating.'

'You'd better start from the beginning. Tell me

absolutely everything.'

*

When Dani glanced around her kitchen, she noted what an eclectic bunch they made. James was home from work and had volunteered to prepare the food.

Andy was pacing about irritably, wanting to stay but worried about getting into hot water with his mother-in-law. Sally was seated at the kitchen table with Rhodri Morgan, both of them enjoying a lively discussion about the sentencing of psychopaths.

Dani called for silence by tapping her wine glass with a teaspoon. 'Thanks for coming. Look, we've all been given the outline of this. Now we need to come up with some proper theories.'

'The man who visited the garage in Sighthill and checked out the Ford Anglia, we're *certain* he wasn't Afro-Caribbean?' Sally asked.

'I've got two witness statements,' Andy replied. 'They both describe the man as a late sixties well-spoken Scotsman with a pale, rugged complexion.'

'It's a shame,' the lawyer continued, 'because it would make sense if Calvin Suter wanted to get rid of that car. He knows the police could try and get forensic evidence off it now and perform a DNA test, which wasn't available at the time of his trial. His guilt would be proved once and for all.'

'*Or* his innocence,' Rhodri put in. 'It makes greater sense to me that someone on the outside got nervous at the idea of Suter's release. The man was hell bent on writing his memoirs and raising the profile of the original murder case once again. I wouldn't be surprised if Suter's legal team weren't looking to locate that car too. Now none of us can lift the evidence that would have been on it. When did these garages holding classic cars start burning to the ground?'

'The first reported arson was at the end of September,' Andy supplied.

'*Before* Suter was even released from prison,' Rhodri stressed.

'It *is* possible that Suter got an associate to do it.' Sally helped herself to more wine. 'We should keep that in mind.'

Andy took a step forward. 'We weren't meant to know that these fires were targeting that specific car. It was a clever plan. Four garages have been burnt, dozens of cars destroyed, but only one was really the target. It's a scheme that required organisation and manpower. I'd be amazed if a single individual could have pulled it off, especially from prison.'

'If there's one thing I know about Calvin, it's that he's a loner. The man doesn't have *associates*, he never has.'

Sally said nothing. Her expression was sceptical.

Dani furrowed her brow. 'How did they find out where the car was?'

'I checked the vehicle's history on the system today,' Andy explained. 'After the trial, it was kept at the police compound in Paisley for six months. Then it got auctioned off to a private owner. This purchaser was the registered keeper until the early eighties. It's been in and out of private car lots since then, turning up at the garage in Sighthill a year ago. The owner thought it was a turkey. He couldn't imagine being able to shift it. That was why the test drive last week really stuck in their minds.'

'How would you find that out if you didn't have access to the police database and the DVLA files?' It was James who asked this question.

'All you need to do is bribe the correct person.' Sally's tone was impatient. 'My investigators have been doing it for years.'

'It's not easy to organise if you're a penniless convict,' Dani retorted.

'Calvin didn't look penniless when I last met him,' Rhodri admitted. 'He's received an advance from a publisher and a hefty payment from a Sunday newspaper.'

Andy put a hand up to halt the debate. 'I've really got to go, but I'll just say this. Somebody out there is trying to destroy evidence from a major crime committed forty years ago. Calvin Suter has already served his time. Every bugger in Scotland believes he did it. He can't get convicted twice over. Why on earth would he want to get rid of that car?' He shook his head vigorously. 'No, it's got to be somebody else. A person who's worried their guilt might be uncovered now that Suter's out and the episode is being re-investigated. If my years as a detective have taught me anything, it's that this bastard is well-connected. He's got access to privileged information *and* money.'

'Which makes him very dangerous,' Dani added, handing him his jacket.

'Exactly,' Andy replied, leaving them to contemplate his words.

Chapter 42

If there was one person who had pre-occupied Calvin Suter's thoughts during the many hours he lay awake on his hard bunk in prison, it was Rick Hunter. On countless occasions, he'd imagined punching his face to a bloody pulp or noisily shagging his wife in front of him, none of which made Calvin feel much better about the terrible betrayal the man had committed.

He and Rick had been friends. Rick had shown him the ropes when he first came to work at Princely Cars in '71. Calvin didn't make friends easily. He was a quiet, reserved person. But Rick was different. He was easy going and never judgemental. Or so he'd thought.

Then the girls started going missing and the police were asking the drivers endless questions. He didn't find out until the evidence was read during his trial that it was Hunter who'd told the police Calvin had a preference for driving the light blue Ford Anglia.

The words were like a dagger through his heart. It was total bullshit. None of the drivers liked being assigned it. Never mind the ridiculous colour, it kept breaking down. More often than not it was locked up in the firm's garage gathering dust. No one gave a crap about where it was or what it was doing the majority of the time. But this piece of sophistry provided a vital chain in the evidence link. Many members of the jury were convinced of Calvin's guilt based on his 'so-called' connection to that rust bucket.

Calvin gazed down at the earth beneath his feet.

'So, this is where you are now, Rick.' He kicked at the soil with his boot. 'It's the one thing I never understood, in all these years. Why did you lie? You were my only friend. Why the hell did you lie?'

He stepped forward and stamped his boot down hard onto the fresh bunch of flowers that had been laid at the foot of the headstone. With all his strength he ground the delicate petals into the dirt.

*

One thing Andy had noticed since DCS Nicholson had retired through ill health was how deathly subdued the serious crime floor now was.

Heads were bent over laptops and the atmosphere was strictly business-like. It wasn't as if they hadn't worked hard before DCS Douglas came along, but there had always been a relaxed atmosphere of joking and camaraderie. No one dared toss a gag at a colleague across a workstation any longer for fear of discovering dour Douglas hovering at their shoulder, ready to slap them with a disciplinary notice.

With the DCI on leave, the place felt even more like a morgue. Calder moved across to Alice Mann's workstation and pulled up a chair. 'How is your investigation into the Abbot woman going?'

'She met with a man yesterday at the St Enoch Centre. I think it may have been Matt Tulloch. Hang on, I took a photo of him on my phone.' Alice showed the screen shot to her colleague.

'Yep, that's him. It must have really shaken him up when the boss and I paid him a visit.'

'The discussion between them didn't look friendly. He left an envelope for Abbot. I'm sure it contained money.'

'She's definitely got a hold over the family.'

'But she's getting weaker with every day, Andy. I'm wondering if the Tullochs know how ill she is. Abbot wore a big coat to the meeting. It covered up her emaciated body completely. Can the woman really be such a threat to them when she's dead?'

'It depends on what the blackmail is about.' Andy dragged a hand through his hair, suddenly deciding to share with Alice the discoveries that Bevan had made about the Suter case and its connection to the recent spate of arson attacks in the city.

The DS leaned back in her seat and whistled. 'You need to track down the man who visited the garage in Sighthill a few days before the fire.'

'All I've got is a description from the garage employees. He gave them a name and address. When I checked it out, the guy looked nothing like the man described and was decades younger. He'd been at work with witnesses when the test drive took place.'

Alice sat up straight again. 'Don't you need a driving licence to take a car out for a test drive?'

Andy nodded slowly. 'It must have been a forgery.'

Alice frowned. 'It's bloody difficult to get hold of a convincing false driving licence, no matter how well connected you are. Especially if you're showing it to someone who handles licences regularly. It would have to be incredibly authentic.'

'What are you suggesting?'

'The licence might have been real. Maybe the man borrowed it from this guy whose name and address he used. I know there's a photo on it, but as long as the picture showed someone who was male and vaguely human the garage owner wasn't going to question it. He just wanted a sale.'

Andy nodded slowly. 'It might be a good idea to go back and speak with this man. Our arsonist must have chosen his name for a reason. Perhaps there's a connection between the two of them.'

Alice picked up her jacket. 'Do you want me to tag along?'

'Of course. You can help me suss him out.'

Chapter 43

As the officers drove out towards Tollcross, Andy took some time to think. He decided that using a false name or taking on somebody else's identity was a bit like choosing a password. You tended to delve back into your history for a reference that held some kind of special significance. Otherwise, you'd never be able to recall it in the future, or, in the case of a criminal, you'd stumble over your lie. False identities often revealed more about a perp than they realised.

Alice parked the car next to a silver people carrier on the driveway. The detectives glanced at one another. The vehicle was clearly being used as a taxi cab. The words; *Fullarton Private Hire* were emblazoned across the side.

Andy leant hard on the doorbell. A bald man in his early forties opened up. 'Hello again, Mr Gillespie. May I come in?'

'I was just about to head out to work.'

'It won't take a moment.' Andy stepped forward into the hallway, forcing the man to retreat backwards. He proceeded into the living room, where the television set was on and a plate of half eaten sausage and beans sat on the coffee table. 'Doesn't look as if you were rushing out of the door, Duncan.'

Duncan Gillespie looked sheepish. 'I was running a bit late.'

Alice leant down and switched the TV off.

'Which job was it that you were heading away to?' Andy made himself comfortable on the sofa. 'The call centre job in the city centre where you told me you were last Monday morning? Or driving the minicab we saw outside?'

Beads of sweat had broken out on the man's bald pate. 'I only do the minicab work during evenings and weekends. My employers don't know about it, but I pay tax on the fares. I swear to it.'

Andy leant forward. 'So if I were to call HMRC right now, they would confirm to me that you are a licenced minicab driver? *And* I assume you have all the necessary insurance and police checks?'

Gillespie began to wring his hands. 'It's only a little side-line. Most of the time I'm ferrying the kids and my old mum about in that thing on the drive.' He attempted a smile, which died on his lips.

Alice decided to intervene. 'Do you know why it's so important to have a licence to drive a minicab, sir? It's because unlicenced cab drivers can prey on young, vulnerable girls with impunity – drive them out to scrubland after picking them up outside a nightclub, abusing the trust they've placed in the driver to deliver them straight home safely.'

Gillespie looked frantic. 'I've never done that! My daughter's fourteen. I'd kill anyone who did something like that to her!'

Andy put out his hand. 'Calm down, Duncan. I'm sure we can get this whole business sorted out. Firstly, we'll need to look at your driving licence.'

He reached for his wallet. 'That's all fine and up-to-date, officer. No problems there.' Gillespie handed the card to Andy.

'You've got a bit more hair in this picture,' Andy chuckled. 'I'm amazed anyone thinks it's you.'

'But it is, see? I only started to thin a couple of years back, now it's all gone. There's no law against that, surely?'

'No,' Alice said calmly. 'But it *is* an offence to allow another individual to use your driving licence. Have you done that recently, sir?'

Sweat was now pouring off the man's face. 'He

said there wouldn't be any trouble! I've got myself totally in the shit now, haven't I?' He glanced pathetically at Andy.

'Not if you can help us out here, Duncan. It's not you we're interested in. It's the man you lent your identity to. Give us his details and we'll be sympathetic about the other crimes.'

*

Dani had prepared her visitors a sandwich. It was the first time that Alice Mann had been inside her boss's flat. She was trying not to be too obvious about taking the place in. It was cosy and nice. Not flashy at all.

'The man we are looking for is a regular client of this Duncan Gillespie?'

'Yes, Gillespie spends most of his time hanging around Prestwick Airport. He never works the pubs and nightclubs, says it's too much hassle having drunks in the car.'

'Most of his clients are businessmen, needing transport into the city centre. That's where he came into contact with Mr Swinton,' Alice explained.

'But we don't think that's his real name?'

'No,' Andy continued. 'Gillespie has known this man for years. He's done various extra-curricular jobs for him. Picking up packages and such like, nothing overtly illegal.'

Alice finished her mouthful and smiled. 'Mr Swinton was aware that Gillespie's taxi work wasn't legit. He knew he could exploit that fact for his own ends. Using Gillespie's name and driving licence last week was just one of those occasions when the man came in useful. Our friend Duncan has provided us with so many addresses; private and business, where he's driven this guy over the years. We're bound to be able to identify him from the information.'

Dani nodded. 'Good.' She sat down at the table with them, gripping her coffee mug. 'This minicab connection must mean something too. It eerily mirrors the Suter case.'

'I've looked into Duncan Gillespie's history closely. There's absolutely no evidence to suggest he uses the cab to molest women.' Andy looked indignant. For some reason, he'd believed the guy on that score.

'No, I'm not thinking along those lines.' Dani glanced at her colleagues. 'How old does Gillespie think that Mr Swinton is?'

Alice responded swiftly, 'Gillespie's been driving the guy around since the mid-nineties. He reckons he was in his early fifties back then.'

'He could be late sixties by now.' Dani lifted the cup to her lips. 'What if this Mr Swinton has been using minicabs for a very long time? Perhaps Duncan Gillespie isn't the first driver he's paid to do little jobs for him. This *is* the man who has gone to enormous lengths to get rid of the blue Ford Anglia, after all.'

Andy nodded. 'I see what you're getting at Ma'am.' The DC downed the rest of his coffee in one mouthful. 'We'd better get back to the station then. Let's find out exactly who this bastard is.'

Chapter 44

Dani wasn't entirely sure if what she was about to do was a good idea. She had driven to Mauchline in Ayrshire straight after lunch. It hadn't taken long to locate the Kilmarnock Road.

The DCI was standing outside the door of the ground floor flat that Rhodri had told her was being rented by Calvin Suter.

The man answered without delay. 'DCI Bevan. This is certainly a surprise.'

'May I come in?'

'Of course.' He stood back graciously, allowing Dani plenty of room to get past.

The house was Victorian and the hallway rather grand. The stairwell had been hidden behind a wall, making the space slightly narrower than it should have been. 'The flat upstairs have their own entrance at the side,' Calvin explained.

He led her into a front sitting room with a large bay window. There were bookshelves on every wall. Dani moved across to glance at some of the titles. 'I notice you have a section dedicated to the work of Samuel Taylor Coleridge. Many of these books look like first editions.'

'He is my favourite poet and writer. My own book was an analysis of his philosophical ideas.' Calvin gestured for Dani to take a seat.

'Is there any reason why you chose Coleridge in particular?'

He smiled. 'I loved any writer who could successfully transport me away from my surroundings, especially as a younger man. Coleridge suffered from depression, did you know?'

Dani shook her head.

'I always sensed he understood what it was like to be imprisoned. I felt it through his words. When I first decided to study English Literature, many of the concepts were completely new to me. Coleridge was the first writer to come up with the notion of *the suspension of disbelief.* Are you familiar with it?'

'That even if something is totally implausible, you have to ignore your doubts for the sake of the plot. We used to use the phrase a lot in essays about Shakespeare's plays.'

Calvin chuckled. 'Yes, so did I. But it held an additional irony for me. Being arrested for the murder of those girls, the subsequent trial and my long incarceration were events so totally bewildering and utterly unlikely that I had to spend forty years *suspending my disbelief.* This was the only way I knew how to accept it really happened. Otherwise, I would have gone quite mad.' He rubbed at his chin. 'I don't expect that makes sense to anyone else.'

'I think I understand.'

Calvin stared at her hard, wrinkling his brow. '*Really*? I stopped believing that anyone would understand how I felt very many years ago.'

'Can I ask you some questions about what went on back in the early seventies? I realise you have every right to refuse.'

Calvin tilted his head. 'Are you actually interested in the truth, DCI Bevan – or in simply discrediting me? I know that you are in a relationship with Jim Irving's son.'

'I am a detective before I am anything else, Mr Suter. If we are going to use literary terms, then that is undoubtedly my fatal flaw. I now have reason to suspect that someone other than yourself murdered those young women between 1972 and 1975. If this fact hurts the people closest to me it won't matter. I will still keep investigating until I find out the truth.'

Calvin's composure had given way slightly. His dark eyes were glistening with moisture. 'Anthony Alderton thought that too. But he was the only one. The younger lawyer, Irving, he always looked at me like I was a monster. My own family disowned me.'

'I know Calvin.' She leant forward. 'Will you help me?'

'What do you want to know?'

'When you were driving the cabs, was there a man a few years older than you, a businessman perhaps; a person who paid the drivers to do things for him. Collect and deliver packages, maybe?'

He sighed deeply. 'It's so long ago, I barely recall. We had a few regular passengers but they tended to be the OAPs who we drove to the shops in Kilmarnock. Because I was one of the youngest and a single man, I always had to cover the pubs and nightclubs at kicking out time. It was the worst shift.'

'Did any of the other drivers have corporate clients who they took to the airport or on the city run, for example?'

A wounded look crossed Calvin's face. 'My *friend* Rick. The one who gave a statement to the police saying I used to drive the Anglia. It was a filthy lie. I never knew why he did it.'

'What about him?'

'Rick was a bit older than me. He had a wife and kids. He always asked the boss for the upmarket clients. He insisted he was the senior driver and had a good way with people. I assumed those customers must give better tips. That's why he wanted them for himself. If anyone at Princely Cars back then had corporate clients, it would have been him.'

'What was his full name?'

'Rick Hunter - Richard, I suppose. He's dead now,

though.'

Dani felt her heart sink. 'Can I ask you one more thing?'

Calvin nodded, looking wary.

'Why did you go to that beach? Did you know that the girls' bodies were hidden there?'

'No, I did not. That beach was my special place. I used to go there whenever I could to get some peace. It reminded me of home – of Montego Bay. It had all the same caves and headlands. If I closed my eyes, I could picture the deep blue of the sky and the sea, feel the warmth of the sun on my face. We'd been happy in Jamaica, before Mum brought us here and started carrying on with all those men. It was hell for me and my sisters after that.'

'Did you ever tell anyone about this special place?'

'I didn't have friends, Detective, not really. I was a withdrawn and ill-educated boy. I couldn't articulate my feelings and desires in the way I can now.' Calvin suddenly gave a start, a memory seeming to force its way into his mind. 'No, that's not true. I had a friend once. He helped me in my new job and encouraged me to talk about myself and the things I loved.' He looked Dani in the eye. 'Yes, I told Rick about the beach and the caves. I told him how peaceful it was, how nobody ever went there, how the caverns were like the catacombs in the cliffs of Montego Bay, where somebody could easily lose themselves forever.'

Chapter 45

Sharing a flat did have its advantages Alice thought, as she dropped her briefcase in the hallway. The lights were on in the living room and the place was warm and cheerful.

She popped her head around the door. Her flatmate, Meera was lying on the sofa with her boyfriend, watching TV. 'Hi Alice! Do you want us to shift up?'

'No, not at all. I'm going to take a shower. You guys go ahead, enjoy the film.'

'There's wine open in the fridge, help yourself!'

Alice smiled as Meera's words followed her up the stairs to her room.

The detective threw herself onto the bed, kicking off her shoes. They were very close to identifying their man. She and Andy had examined the employee records of every single company that Duncan Gillespie had driven Mr Swinton to since 1995. Only one name had cropped up in them all. It had positively jumped out at them, in fact.

Andy was also trying to track down the physical evidence from the trial of Calvin Suter in October 1975. At first, the records department said they couldn't find it. Then a manager came back off his lunchbreak and claimed to know where the stuff may be. When she left the department, Calder was still waiting to lay his hands on it.

Alice was very nearly asleep when the phone began buzzing by her side. It took a moment for her to shake her thoughts back to reality and answer it.

'DS Mann? This is the Oncology Department at the Glasgow Infirmary. We had your details on file regarding an inquiry into the health of Ms Lisa Abbot?'

'Yes, that's correct.' Alice was immediately alert.

'I'm sorry to bother you, Sergeant. Your number was literally all we had in relation to this patient. There are no surviving family or friends.'

'Has something happened?'

'Ms Abbot was rushed into the ICU this afternoon. Her condition has seriously worsened. We believe the cancer may have reached her respiratory system. We don't think she has very long.'

'I'll be there in half an hour. Thank you for calling.'

*

Alice had dressed casually. She didn't want this visit to appear official. One of the specialists accompanied the sergeant to the room where Lisa was occupying a bed, connected to a respirator.

'Can she still talk?' Alice tried to keep the alarm out of her voice.

'Yes, the breathing tube is just a precaution, to make her feel more comfortable. Lisa has been given morphine to manage the pain. She's drifting in and out of consciousness.'

'How long do you think she's got?'

'We can never tell in these situations. Hours possibly, a few days perhaps. No longer than that.'

'Lisa was banking on being able to go to America, to try this new drug that they've developed over there. It's a shame she hasn't managed to hold out long enough to make the trip.'

The doctor smiled wistfully. 'It's a blessing, Sergeant. The drug that Lisa had found out about on the internet was in the early stages of its trials on patients. There were some astonishing initial results, but this can often be put down to other factors. It would have been a long and painful road for her. In my opinion, she was simply delaying the inevitable and would have died in a foreign land, far away from everything she knew and loved.'

Alice doubted whether Lisa Abbot loved anything or anyone. 'Can I go in?'

'You aren't going to upset her?' The doctor suddenly looked worried.

'No, of course not. I've been watching her for so long that I've come to feel as if I know her well. Do you understand what I mean?'

He nodded, smiling. 'In the end, our common humanity will always unite us.'

Alice shook his hand warmly before entering the overheated room. She shrugged off her cardigan and sat by the bedside. 'Lisa, can you hear me?'

The woman turned her pale face. A flicker of recognition showed in her eyes. Lisa lifted her hand, as if she were trying to tug at the tube.

'Would you like to speak?'

She nodded weakly.

Alice gently pulled the mask from the woman's mouth, waiting for her breathing to become regular again. 'How are you feeling?'

'What are you doing here?' Lisa rasped.

'The doctors called me. Mine was the only number they had. Don't you have any family, Lisa? Can I contact someone to be here with you?'

'No. There's nobody.'

'What about from the time when you were still Sara White? That is your *real* name, isn't it? Where are your parents, your siblings?'

Her body stiffened and her breathing became more ragged. Alice glanced worriedly at the monitors. She didn't want the doctors rushing in. 'Okay. We don't need to talk about that. Tell me something else instead. There was a picture of you in your flat. It was very sunny and you were with a young man. It seemed like a happy time.'

Lisa's body relaxed. 'It was.'

'Where were you both? It looked tropical.'

'Fiji. We stayed there for a year.'

'Who was with you? He seemed nice. Handsome.'

'That's Matt. He was my boyfriend.'

'But not any longer?'

'He hates me now.'

Alice touched her arm, shocked by how cold the skin was. 'I'm sure that can't be true. I could call him? Ask him to come?'

'No, it's too late.'

'Did you meet Matt when you were working for the Tulloch family?'

Lisa nodded her head and coughed. 'Matt's mum thought he was too young for me, so they sent me away. She was angry, called me awful things.'

'But Matt followed you?'

A tear slid down the woman's cheek. 'When he turned sixteen, he came to join me. We took a flight to the South Pacific and I supported us, by working in bars and hotels. It was the happiest time of my whole life.'

'What went wrong?'

'Matt got bored. He was just a little rich boy all along. By the time his Dad tracked us down in our little beach house in Fiji, he was ready to go home. The game was over.'

'I'm sorry. But why does Matt hate you, shouldn't it be the other way around if he was the one who left?'

Lisa shifted her head to one side. 'I know things.'

Alice felt her heart beat faster. 'What do you know, Lisa?'

The woman turned slowly back to face her visitor.

'I can tell you things, terrible things, but I want something in return.'

'What do you want?' Alice wondered what this dying woman could possibly need or desire with so little time left in this world.

'I want to see my daughter.'

Chapter 46

DCS Douglas looked oddly out of place in dark chino trousers and an open-necked shirt. He was deep in conversation with Brian Tulloch in the waiting area of the Oncology Department. For the first time, Dani was mightily thankful she wasn't a member of senior management.

'*Jeez*, I wouldn't like to be in Douglas's shoes.' Andy whistled through his teeth.

'He's definitely taking one for the team there.' Dani glanced towards the window of the hospital room, where Glenda and Ellie Tulloch were seated by Lisa's bedside. The scene appeared amicable enough.

Alice returned from the machine with their coffees. 'I honestly didn't think they'd come.'

'The woman is dying. I suspect that swung it for Glenda Tulloch. When we broke the news to her at the house earlier, about Lisa's terminal cancer, I could see how relieved she was. All this time they've been worried that Lisa would take Ellie back. That's what she's been holding over them for the last thirteen years. Abbot had the power to make the Tullochs do anything she pleased.'

'Do you believe that's why she had the baby in the first place?' Andy asked.

'I don't think so,' Alice replied. 'Sara – as she was then, discovered she was pregnant when they were hiding out in Fiji. Brian Tulloch found Matt, Sara and Ellie living together on the beach. It was a pretty squalid existence. Matt had had enough of his little adventure by then and wanted to go home. There was never any question that Ellie would go with them. Matt was only fourteen when Sara began a sexual relationship with him. She was working as Fran's au pair at the time. As far as the Tullochs were concerned, the girl was a child molester. They didn't want the shame of the whole pitiful episode coming out, nor the risk that their grandchild would stay in her care.'

'Did Sara object to them taking Ellie?'

'No, they offered her money, lots of it. Sara was to disappear and allow the Tulloch's to raise Ellie as their daughter. She *was* their own flesh and blood after all.'

'Sara changed her name to Lisa Abbot, using the two identities to extort money from people.'

'But she maintained her hold over the Tullochs. Lisa thought it would be useful to be able to drive Glenda's car from time to time. So she demanded that her name go on the insurance.'

'No wonder Mrs Tulloch was so determined to take the rap for the vehicle offences. She was desperate not to lose her little girl.'

'Lisa was squeezing what she could out of the Tullochs until the very last moment. I saw her receiving money from Matt again the other day in town,' Alice added. 'She'd tried to hide the fact she was ill. I don't think he had a clue.'

'Did you feel sorry for Lisa? Is that why we've granted her this final wish?'

The corner of Alice's lip curled up. 'Not at all. That woman has got information. I want to know exactly who's responsible for the deaths of Raymond and Janet Kerr. I want to hear her admit that she killed poor Kath Nevin. I never dreamed I'd get something like this to use as leverage with her - not a dying woman with nothing to lose.'

'Who knew Lisa Abbot actually had feelings for the daughter she sold to her in-laws and had no proper contact with for the following thirteen years.'

'I don't think she knew herself, Andy. Not until the woman realised she was about to kick the bucket.'

Chapter 47

Alice stood in the doorway and motioned for the visitors to leave.

'No! I want them to stay longer. I want to see Ellie on her own!' Lisa's face was amazingly defiant, considering how weak she was.

'I'll see what I can do. But we need to have a chat first.' Alice waited for Glenda and Ellie to reach the corridor before she pulled the door shut. 'Now, Lisa. I've done what you asked. It's time to tell me what you know. It will make you feel better to talk, make the passing easier, I promise.'

Lisa relaxed back against the pillows, her breaths coming slow and regular. 'I needed the money for my treatment in the States. Ray was always happy to help out, but he didn't have much. Really, I needed more. It was Janet's savings and compensation money that I wanted.'

'How did you plan to get it?'

Lisa let out a humourless laugh. 'I made a mistake. I decided to tell the truth, for the first time in my bloody life! I called Ray on the Wednesday night and told him I had cancer. That he needed to ask his mum for the money to pay for my treatment. I knew she had it in her account. But Ray became distressed and incoherent. I thought maybe he didn't understand what I was telling him, how serious it was. So I asked a friend to visit them both on the following evening. He was to pretend to be my doctor, tell them how I didn't have long to live without the treatment. That was all.'

'Who was this friend?'

'Nick McKenna. He wasn't prepared to give me

the money, so I told him he had to do this little job for me instead. Nick swears that when he left the Kerrs' place, they were upset but still alive.'

'He never told us this.'

'No, he asked me to sort it. He'd get his wife to release the money if I made sure that nobody ever knew he visited the house in Anniesland on the night they died.'

'Then we got the statement from Kath Nevin.'

'I've got contacts on that street. I heard about the police asking questions, producing an E-fit, for Christ's sake. Without the witness, there could be no further action taken. I knew Mrs Nevin's little habits. You could've set your watch by her. It was easy enough to follow the old bag to the bus stop. She wasn't very careful when she crossed that busy road.'

Alice stood up. 'And no one to your knowledge returned to the Kerrs' property on that night?'

'No, that was it. Nick was the only one there.'

'Thank you Lisa, that's all I needed to know.'

'What about Ellie – is she coming back in?'

Alice snorted incredulously. 'Goodbye Ms Abbot.'

'Wait.' She grabbed Alice's sleeve. 'There's something else. We always went sailing a lot.'

'Who did?'

'When I worked for the Tullochs. Brian was running the yacht club at Tighnabruaich in those days. We went there most weekends during the summer.'

'Why is this of any conceivable interest to me?' Alice wanted to shake the woman's hand off her shirt.

'Brian had lots of business friends. Every weekend there was some new guy on the yacht. They all looked at me like they wanted to rip my clothes off. But one man was different. I think he noticed something in me. He spoke to me like I was his equal. I liked him.'

'What was his name?'

'Gregory.'

Alice's body stiffened. She lowered herself back into the chair. 'Tell me about him.'

'One Saturday afternoon it was very hot. The sun was beating down onto the deck of the boat. The Tullochs had been drinking all day with their guests. Gregory asked me to sit next to him. I don't think Brian minded much. He wanted to keep his clients happy and I was nothing to him. Gregory was a bit old for me, he was in his fifties. I don't reckon he fancied me, just wanted to talk. It seemed to give him a thrill to whisper all these terrible, horrific things to me.'

'What did he say?'

'Gregory told me about that stretch of coastline. How it contained dozens of little caves and caverns. He said that some of them stretched for miles into the hillsides. He liked to visit them by boat, that way you could discover a tiny headland that maybe nobody else even knew existed. I said that was bullshit. It was Scotland, not bloody darkest Africa. So he said, if it was bullshit, how come nobody knew about the cave where he'd hidden the bodies?'

Alice took in a sharp breath. 'What bodies?' Her voiced sounded weaker than Lisa's.

'Of all the women he'd tortured and killed. Gregory had money and connections. He said it was easy enough to find girls. They spilled out of clubs and pubs every night of the week. Sometimes he borrowed a taxi cab to pick them up, other times he chatted them up in a bar. Whichever took his fancy. Then he lured them into his car and drove them out to the coast. He drugged them and sailed them to his little cave in a boat. It was perfect, he said. Nobody could interrupt him. He was like Neptune. Out there amongst the waves where his power was absolute.'

'Would you be able to show us on a map where this place is, Lisa?' Alice knew how frantic she sounded. They had to know that location, before it was too late.

'It was a long time ago.'

'But can you please try? I could organise for Ellie to come in again. We could leave you alone this time?'

Lisa made a monumental effort to lift her head up from the pillow. There was a triumphant look on her face. 'I knew this information was good. The best I've ever had. But there wasn't very much I could do with it until now. It's a shame there was never any money to be made out of it.'

Alice had to breathe in deeply and count to ten, otherwise she was likely to reach forward and throttle the woman, deathbed or not. 'I'm going to get my DCI. We'll come back in a wee while with a map of the Argyle and Bute coastline. I want you to pinpoint where Gregory told you this cave was situated. Then you can see Ellie.'

Lisa lay back down and pouted. 'Okay, you win.'

Chapter 48

The weather didn't even have the decency to be bad. A piercing autumn sun was spilling over the mountains of Bute and making the water in the bay sparkle.

The police launch had been powering along the straights for some time. They'd passed through the remote waterways of Loch Ruel and Loch Riddon. This was territory that Dani had not entered into before.

She glanced at Alice sitting beside her, wrapped up in her padded coat and life jacket. The young woman's wide eyes scoured every contour of this jagged coastline, only breaking the search to look down every so often at the map, protected by a plastic sleeve and gripped firmly in both her hands.

'We'll find it,' Dani said quietly.

'I wish we could have made her come with us, to point out exactly where the place is.'

'She was never going to last that long. It's a miracle she ever told us about what Gregory said to her all those years ago. Lisa Abbot had no conscience to speak of. That's down to you.' Dani rested her hand on Alice's arm.

The young sergeant shrugged off the praise. 'You or Andy would have done the same.'

Dani gazed out at the dark silhouettes of the hills, with the bright sun framed behind them. 'I'm not so sure about that. You found a way to get through to Lisa. She opened up to you like no one else.'

'I'm not convinced that's a virtue, Ma'am.'

Dani smiled but said nothing.

The boat seemed to have entered some kind of swell. There was barely any wind so it had no obvious cause.

'Is everything okay up there, Tam?' Dani called to the Skipper.

'Aye, we're just entering a stretch of water where the currents are notoriously strong. Think of it as like your Grannie stirring her porridge.'

Dani gripped the gunwales as the launch pitched from left to right. Despite the instability of the boat, Alice suddenly leapt to her feet. 'I think it's over there Ma'am.' She pointed towards a rocky headland to the west.

'Can we reach it, Tam?'

'I'll do my best, but these swells wouldn't make it a likely tourist spot.'

'That's exactly the kind of location we're looking for.'

Eventually, Tam brought the launch into a tiny cove. There was nowhere to tie up. He recommended they get as close as possible to the shore and wade in from there.

The DCI nodded her agreement.

Alice, Dani and a DC from Tighnabruaich made their way steadily towards the cliffs. They had torches and ropes, which the DC secured to a boulder before they began to investigate the cave system itself.

The tide was low enough for them to splash through the main cave to reach a smaller opening at the back. 'We're going to have to crawl in,' Dani instructed her colleagues, who were taking up the rear.

With her torch held out in front, the DCI led the way along a smooth, damp tunnel. The gradient abruptly shelved and she found herself deposited unceremoniously on the hard shingle in a smaller, darker cave which lay beyond. A few minutes later, Alice dropped down beside her.

They allowed their torches to travel across the sides of the cavern. Dani took a couple of steps further inside, pointing the beam into a scooped out section of rock, its ceiling lower than the rest of the chamber.

Dani gasped. The light revealed the glint of metal.

Alice jogged over to take a closer look. 'They're chains, Ma'am.'

They both fell deadly silent as they surveyed the full scene, perfectly aware of exactly what they were looking at; piles and piles of jumbled, discoloured, but perfectly intact, human remains.

Dani felt the bile rise to the back of her throat and the tears sting her eyes. 'We got it wrong, Alice. For *forty* fucking years we got it so wrong.'

Chapter 49

Dani stood side by side with DCS Douglas, watching the interview through the wall of glass.

'This is big, Danielle. Totally fucking huge.'

She'd never heard Ronnie Douglas swear before. It almost made her laugh out loud. 'Compensation will have to be paid to Calvin, certainly. It could run into the millions.'

'It's not just that. This guy,' he pointed a long finger at the man seated directly ahead of them. 'Has friends in very high places. Some extremely important people are going to look like fools when this gets out. That's not good news for the rest of us.'

'But think of the families, sir. We've got at least seven missing persons, including Sarah Martin in 1978, who's bodies can be returned to their parents. I'm convinced there was another victim between Kirsty Glendinning and Debbie Cane. The gap between the two killings was just too large. It didn't fit the perpetrator's established pattern.'

'Then we're talking about victims going back forty years who may never have been reported missing. It's a massive task for the forensic pathologists.'

'And my team will assist them all the way.'

Douglas turned to face her. 'I want you to handle all the media interviews related to this. You're going to make up for the colossal cock-ups of the past.'

'Of course, sir.'

Dani silently observed Alice and Andy at work. They were delivering the evidence the team had mounted against this man piece by tiny piece. The DCI could see Gregory Suter's smug face slowly crumpling as he absorbed the inevitable truth.

They'd got him.

'So Calvin never knew about his father's family?' Douglas said quietly.

'No. Calvin's dad was a Scottish businessman who was based in Jamaica for a few years in the 1950s. According to our research, Billy Suter had illegitimate children dotted around the globe. He had a weakness for *exotic* women. All the time, he had a respectable family back in Glasgow that he eventually returned home to. Suter provided Calvin's mum with money for a while, but it soon petered out.'

'How did Gregory find out about Calvin?'

'Professor Morgan believes that Gregory always knew about his father's behaviour. It would explain his murderous hatred of those he considered to be *loose* women.'

'The women who he felt were to blame for enticing his father to betray his mother and ruining their family life, destroying his father's 'good name'.'

'Gregory would have despised their illegitimate offspring even more. They diluted what he considered to be special about his privileged family unit – they might even have threatened to take *his* place in his father's affections.'

'Calvin never set out to do any of those things.'

'That's right. Gregory was a young man, starting out in his father's business back in the seventies. But he already possessed his perverted and murderous urges. Gregory was a regular client of a taxi driver for Princely Cars called Rick Hunter. He paid Hunter to do various tasks for him, including allowing the man to use the blue Ford Anglia to pick up his victims.'

'I thought the car was unreliable. Couldn't Hunter have done better?'

'Not really. Any other of the cars would have been

immediately missed. The Anglia sat in the garage most of the time. None of the drivers ever wanted to take it out. The problems started for both men when the police received the witness statements identifying the car at the scene of two abductions. It turned the spotlight on the employees at the firm, including Hunter. This was when the police surveillance started.'

'So Hunter pointed the finger at Calvin, instead. He gave a sworn statement to the police saying it was Calvin who usually drove that car. It was a fabrication, but Hunter had no obvious reason to lie. He had an alibi for all the murders.'

'Do we think that Gregory instructed Hunter to frame his half-brother?'

'I believe it's very likely. Calvin told Hunter about the caves in Ayrshire. Hunter passed the information onto Gregory who used them as his murder site. Then they had the extraordinary good fortune of Calvin leading the police to the bodies. They must have been rubbing their hands with glee. Calvin would get the blame and Gregory would simply find another place to take his victims.'

'What was in it for Hunter – did he play a part in the raping and murdering of the girls?'

'I think for him it was about the money. He turned a blind eye to everything else. But Hunter's dead now, so we'll never know.'

'It was Gregory Suter's wealth and connections that kept him undetected for so long. He had Hunter in his pocket forty years ago and he's still doing it now. He bought off that cabbie in Fullarton and employed those thugs to burn down the garages and destroy crucial evidence for him. Just who the hell does he think he is?' The DCS brought his fist down hard against the frame of the window. The vibrations seemed to rock the foundations of the building itself.

Dani considered her boss's words for a moment. She stared levelly at the seated figure of Gregory Alan Suter, 68 years of age, dressed in a dark grey suit with a striped shirt underneath and a college tie at the neck.

Douglas was right. Who was this man? Because to Dani, he looked pretty damned ordinary.

Chapter 50

For a man who was instrumental in solving one of the biggest cases in Scottish history, Dani didn't think her colleague looked very happy.

She slapped him on the back. 'Come on Andy, drink up. I want to get another round in.'

'I've had enough, thanks.' Andy let his gaze drop to the bottom of the beer glass.

Alice nudged his elbow. 'We should be celebrating. The evidence bag that you searched police storage rooms the length and breadth of western Scotland for has come back from forensics with a match. Gregory Suter's DNA was all over Cheryl Moss's clothes. That's the clincher. Even the best lawyers money can buy can't wriggle him out of that one.'

'Aye, it's good news.' Andy downed the remainder of his pint.

'Then why do you look like you've picked up a penny and lost a tenner, eh?'

Andy eyed each of his colleagues in turn. 'Because I've worked out what happened to the Kerrs, that's why.'

Alice stopped smiling. 'We know what happened. Lisa told them about her cancer and Nick McKenna gave them all the gory details. They couldn't take any more of the pressure for money and the pair took their own lives. It was awful, but nothing's changed.'

'Everything's bloody changed.'

Dani leant forward. 'What are you thinking, Andy?'

He sighed. 'The crime scene and pathologist's

report never really made sense to me. But I can see it all now, in full bloody technicolour.

Lisa calls Ray and tells him she's going to die without getting thousands of pounds from somewhere for the newest treatment, right? Ray's a simple soul and he loves her. He never had the slightest inkling she was a fraud. So he's brooding on this piece of information for another twenty four hours. Then laughing boy turns up at the door claiming to be Lisa's doctor. He lays it on with a trowel about her needing this specialist treatment. Ray's going to be pretty distraught by this point, yeah? But his mum? I reckon Janet's had enough of it. She's been getting it in the ear from her sister and hasn't the slightest intention of parting with her life savings for a scrag-end like Abbot.'

'Oh God.' Dani rested her head in her hands. 'After McKenna had gone, Ray begged his mum to give him the money for Lisa's treatment. But she said no. In fact, she was adamant - Lisa Abbot wasn't going to get any more money out of them, especially her husband's compensation.'

Andy nodded grimly. 'In a fit of grief, anger and frustration, Ray held his mother's arms and poured bleach down her throat. He restrained her until she struggled no longer. Those bruises on her skin weren't from the coffee table at all. They were caused by her son.'

'And like a child, he quickly recovered from his tantrum and realised what he'd done. He took some barbiturates which he had in the bathroom cabinet to help him sleep and swallowed the rest of the bleach himself.'

They sat in silence for a while, listening to the cheerful chatter of their fellow drinkers.

Then Dani spoke. 'It may not have happened that way. We can't be certain.'

'*Oh* it did, Ma'am. We all know it.'

Alice narrowed her eyes so the pupils were like tiny black dots behind her lashes. 'If Lisa Abbot wasn't already dead and buried, I'd ring her flaming neck.'

Three Months Later

Dani's tiny garden lay under a thin layer of snow. The DCI turned back from the window. 'What's the temperature like in Montego Bay?'

James checked his smartphone. '27°'

Dani smiled. 'How lovely.'

He moved across to stand behind her, slipping his arms around her waist. 'Do you know if Calvin has settled in okay?'

'Rhodri is flying out to visit him at the end of the month. We'll find out then. But I expect so. I've seen photos of the beach house. It looks absolutely gorgeous.'

James pressed his face into her neck. 'I hope he's blissfully happy there. He should have enough money to live very comfortably. But can it possibly make up for losing forty years of his life?'

'No, it can't. Calvin must be careful not to allow any feelings of bitterness and regret to ruin the time he has left. Rhodri will help him with that, I'm sure.'

Dani twisted her head. 'What about your dad? How is he doing these days?'

'Not wallowing in bitterness and regret, thankfully. He and Mum are going on a cruise in a couple of weeks. Meeting with Calvin during the trial really helped him a lot. I think Dad realises now that there was no choice back in '75 but for Calvin to plead innocent, because that's exactly what he was. It turns out Sir Anthony Alderton wasn't the insensitive clod we always thought.'

'It shows how important a good legal defence really is. Sometimes the police get it wrong. Terribly, tragically wrong.'

'Tell that to Sally. She's gone all moralistic since this whole Suter affair. Did you know she's dropped the Aaron Lister case?'

Dani shook her head. 'I didn't know that. Why?'

'Because she says he's an arrogant, high-handed sexual predator. He used his position of authority to abuse the students in his care. Sally is refusing to represent him or discredit his victims.'

'But he may not have done it. I'll never be as sure now about someone's guilt as I have been in the past.'

'Well, if he is, another lawyer is going to have to put that case forward in court. They won't be half as good at their job as Sally, that's for sure.'

'Oh, I nearly forgot.' Dani slipped out of James's arms and moved across to the kitchen, picking up the morning paper from the worktop. 'Rhodri is quoted on the front page. He's commenting on the arrest of the university sex attacker, saying that psychological profiling and good old fashioned police work led to his capture.'

James placed his hand gently on her shoulder. 'Has the man admitted to the attack on you in the library toilets?'

Dani shook her head. 'No. He's denied knowing anything about it. But I'm not surprised.' She looked her boyfriend in the eye. 'It was Gregory Suter, or one of his hired heavies, who attacked me that day. He knew I'd been digging into the '75 murders. He was probably having Calvin watched and knew I'd met with him and Rhodri. The attack was exactly as I believed it to be. It was a warning to stay away from the case.'

James pulled her to him again. 'He's locked up now. Gregory Suter will die in prison. The whole thing is over.'

Dani sighed. 'I'm just thinking about Sarah

Martin's funeral. Her sister was there and Ed Callan and his wife. But her poor parents didn't live to see their daughter buried. The same goes for several of the other victims. A few we haven't even identified yet. He was free for too long, James. The police failed a lot of girls and families.'

'The man was clever and well-connected. You said yourself that he spread out his killing sprees and remained dormant for years at a time. This made detection less likely.'

'And reduced the number of victims. It could have been even worse.' Dani touched his face. 'They should have caught him in '78 though. Sarah Martin was one of the secretaries who worked for Gregory Suter at his financial services company in the city. It must have been him she was meeting that night in the bar in Fenwick. He was only in his thirties back then and could attract young women easily. Sarah may have suspected that her boyfriend was seeing another woman during his trips away, so she began a fling with her boss. Sarah had no idea how unsafe this liaison would be.'

'Was Gregory Suter questioned by police at the time?'

'Yes, but only in the most perfunctory way. He had an alibi of course. Several witness statements said he was at his club in Glasgow on the night Sarah disappeared. We know now that those people would have been paid to lie.'

'He was probably charismatic and plausible. I can imagine why he slipped through the net.'

'I watched Gregory Suter very carefully during the trial. Actually, I thought he was strikingly ordinary. You would pass him in a crowd without giving him a second glance.'

'Don't they say that's the hallmark of true evil? That in fact, the form it takes can be rather banal.

Just look at Hitler, or Stalin.'

Dani smiled and nuzzled his cheek. 'I'd rather look at you.'

He chuckled.

'Are you content to stay here in Glasgow with a mere Detective Chief Inspector? Alice is bound to get promotion this month. She'll probably progress faster through the ranks than I will now.'

'Does it matter? I rather like things the way they are. Your boss didn't turn out to be quite as much of a fiend as you first thought.'

'No, he's growing on me. But his most unlikely new pal is Andy Calder. The fact that Andy managed to connect the garage arson attacks to Gregory Suter and the Ford Anglia from the '75 murders has been viewed as the moment the case was cracked. Douglas has been parading him around every newsroom in Glasgow.'

'I bet Andy's really enjoying that. He loves the press.'

Dani laughed. 'You'd be surprised how well Calder can turn on the charm when he needs to. I'm pleased for him. He deserved some credit for once.'

'Then let's take a step back and allow the others to soak up the limelight. I might take you away for a little holiday, DCI Bevan. A *proper* one this time.'

'Okay, Mr Irving. That sounds great.'

*

It was impossible to describe the clear blue of the ocean that stretched out in front of him, so Calvin didn't even try. He'd not written a single word since arriving in Montego Bay a few weeks before.

He sat on the smooth yellow sand in his bare feet and allowed the sun to warm his face. He'd been there for some time when he felt something warm and wet nuzzling his toes.

'I'm so sorry.'

Calvin opened his eyes. A lady was standing with her back to the light, pulling a handsome dog away by its lead. 'Not to worry, no harm done.'

'He likes people, that's all.'

Calvin smiled. 'It must be nice to have the company.'

'Yes, it is. I'm on my own now. I always bring my friend here on trips. Some countries don't like it, but Jamaica is very accommodating.'

'We are a laid back people.'

The lady tilted her head and eyed him closely. 'Are you local? You've got a very strong Scottish accent.'

Calvin laughed. 'I was born here. Now I've come home to retire. What about you? Are you English?'

She nodded. 'Milton Keynes. Not the most beautiful location in the world, is it! That's why I travel. I realised I'd not seen enough places. I'm staying at the Caribbean Beach Hotel, just along the shore. It's very pleasant.'

'Have you been to Jamaica before?'

'Oh yes, several times. But I always stay in the resort. The tour operators say that's best.'

Calvin got to his feet. 'Oh, that's nonsense. All

you need is a decent guide. This coastline is full of beautiful beaches and headlands. It's a wonderful area to explore.'

She hesitated for a second. 'Perhaps you could show me some of these places? Sorry, I'm being very forward. It's just that at my age you find there's no point in wasting time.'

Calvin nodded. 'Don't apologise. I'd love to show you the sights and I agree. We are in paradise. I have absolutely no intention of wasting a single moment.'

The Garansay Press

If you enjoyed this novel, please take a few moments to write a brief review. Reviews really help to introduce new readers to my books and this allows me to keep on writing.
Many thanks,

Katherine.

If you would like to find out more about my books and read my reviews and articles then please visit my blog, TheRetroReview at:

www.KatherinePathak.wordpress.com

To find out about new releases and special offers follow me on Twitter:

@KatherinePathak

Most of all, thanks for reading!

© Katherine Pathak, 2015

≈

The Garansay Press

Made in the USA
San Bernardino, CA
11 October 2016